THE
HEAVEN
STONE

☙☙☙☙☙☙☙☙☙

THE
HEAVEN
STONE

DAVID DANIEL

A THOMAS · DUNNE BOOK

ST. MARTIN'S PRESS
NEW YORK

Design by Ellen R. Sasahara

Library of Congress Cataloging-in-Publication Data

Daniel, David.
    The heaven stone / David Daniel.
      p. cm.
    "A Thomas Dunne book."
    ISBN 0-312-11282-3
    1. Private investigators—Massachusetts—Lowell—Fic-
tion. 2. Cambodian Americans—Massachusetts—Lowell—
Fiction. 3. Lowell (Mass.)—Fiction. I. Title.
    PS3554.A5383H43   1994
    813'.54—dc20   94-19817
                                         CIP

First edition: October 1994

10 9 8 7 6 5 4 3 2 1

For my brothers, Jack and Mark.
And for the gang at Tamarack

Thanks to John Cosner, Jane Gentry,
Jonathan Matson, Robert Sanchez, and
Tim Trask, who saw this novel in an early
stage and were encouraging.

THE
HEAVEN
STONE

1

〇〇〇〇〇〇〇〇〇

*How do you tell yet another story that begins in a
barroom and ends in a graveyard? You say, listen:*

"HEY, PALLY."
The woman's voice came out of the dimness. The place
was a cave on Middlesex Street with graffiti on the walls,
like messages from an ancient past—warnings maybe, to
stay away. But I was impervious. I was working.
"Over here, pally."
I looked over my shoulder for a guy with a pocketbook
maybe, but the entire party at eight o'clock in the morning
was a woman, an unshaven barkeep stocking a cooler
chest, and me. I'd been called a lot of things by a lot of
people, but *pally* wasn't one of them.
"You him?" the woman said as I got nearer. "You Alex
Rasmussen?"
I said I was. "Rita?"
She raised an empty beer glass. "Thaz me."
My eyes were adjusting. Too much bleach had turned
her hair into a bird's nest, and despite the makeup, her
complexion was sallow. But she featured one of those
shapes that could work in the foldout of a magazine, the

kind they kept in shrink-wrap behind the counter at Quick-Mart. It better be this month's issue, though—she looked like she was hitting something pretty hard, and I didn't think it came in a bottle.

"Siddown, pally, buy yourself a beer. Buy me one too. Lez party."

"Give her a coffee," I told the barman.

He shot me a look and kept loading bottles. "You want croissants too?"

His pronunciation wasn't great, but I gave him that one. He uncapped another High Life and set it in front of her. When he'd gone back to work, I said to the woman, "Did you bring the goodies?"

"Did you?"

I took the packet out of my suitcoat pocket and laid it on the bar. She reached for it, but I kept my hand on top. Grumbling, she got a large brown envelope from under her pocketbook and shoved it at me.

I opened it and fingered through the eight-by-tens inside, then sealed it again. She was counting the cash, but I think the number of bills threw her off. Her fine-motor skills didn't seem too acute. "What's this?" she said when she came to my note. "Who the hell's Tony Rossi?"

Her acting was no better than her math. "Just give it to him." I put a couple singles on the bar for the beer.

The woman turned jerkily and clamped a hand on my arm. "Hey, how 'bout that party? I can get us a room upstairs." Her smile was like the vacancy sign outside a cheap motel; she wasn't wasting any neon on the "no".

"I'm not a morning person," I said. "And you better tell Rossi you want a bigger cut if you've got to be doing his job for him."

Her pet name for me wasn't pally anymore.

My eyes winced at the raw sunlight outside. I turned left

2

on Middlesex, walking past barrooms exhaling their dank breath into the cool morning, past flophouses and storefront churches, junkies and hookers and bums, passing no judgment. Years of working with cops and lawyers taught forbearance.

The phonebooth-sized waiting room outside my office was empty. Undaunted, I made coffee, then called the political candidate whose money I had just spent. "In ten minutes they're in the mail," I told him.

"Sweet mother of God, is this really the last of it?"

"You have any other daughters?"

I told him I was personally going to carry the envelope across the street and mail it when the post office opened. He said he couldn't thank me enough. I told him that a check would be a step in the right direction. The candidate laughed the laugh of the relieved and hung up.

I stood looking out the window like a king in my own little empire where the sun never set. Day or night I could look up and there it was. These days the newspaper is actually printed directly across the street, at 15 Kearney Square, but my third-floor streetfront office at number 10 looked kitty-corner on the original building with the three big letters on the roof, ten floors up.

The eight-by-tens lay on my otherwise clear desk, samples from a figure studies class that must have been held off-campus one day. The candidate had not gone to the police because then the blackmail try would have been news, and there would be ten other people in line looking for a lever. The young woman in the black-and-whites was the candidate's daughter, three years ago when she was an art student in Boston. They weren't all that naughty by some standards, but these days she was running dad's campaign.

The blackmailer, I'd discovered, was an ex-classmate of

3

hers and sometime pimp named Tony Rossi, who had gotten the negatives. My client had hinted that maybe I could knuckle the guy's head, but I convinced him that that kind of behavior was best kept on the statehouse floor—though I did give him an option clause should any more threats appear.

That done, it meant I'd caught up on my caseload: not hard to do since it was the only job I'd had all month. I had a standing offer from a guy I knew at Raytheon to come walk rounds with a Detex clock. I hadn't taken him up yet. It was only July tenth.

So I stood at the window gazing out across the intersection of East Merrimack and Bridge streets, meditating on the fall of empire and how easy it was to talk people out of their clothes when a knock on the door jarred the chain of thought.

Most people approach that outer door as if it might hit back. Most are doing it for the first and only time, so they're edgy about why they've come. Seeing my name with INVESTIGATOR under it probably hurts as much as it helps. So my ear is tuned to soft knocks, quiet knocks, timorous, tentative, hesitant, apologetic knocks, maybe-I-should-forget-the-whole-thing knocks. This was another kind. The butt-end of a cop's flashlight knock, an "Open up, we know you're in there!" knock. I opened.

I had to drop my gaze a foot to see the woman standing there.

"Mr. Rasmussen?" she said in a soft voice.

"Yes."

"My name is Ada Stewart. May I talk to you?"

No one that good-looking had asked that question in months. I got her inside and settled into the chair in front of my desk. I covered the pictures on the blotter and of-

4

fered coffee from the vintage Joe DiMaggio autograph-model Mr. Coffee. She demurred politely, and I warmed my own cup. I was sorry I didn't have any green tea to offer: she was some part Asian, a generation or two removed; Chinese if I had to guess, but with a last name like Stewart, no trace of accent, and round-eye mixed in, a guess is all it would be. I'd have said thirty, but it could have gone up or down by a few. She missed petite because she was full-figured, with thick black hair that tickled the knob at the base of her neck. She wore a pink blouse, a simple black skirt, nylons, and shoes as glossy as licorice. The fragrance that came with her, so subtle it reached me only now, was jasmine. Maybe the drumming on the door had been an effort to control the slight tremor I saw in the hands she curled in her lap. She wore no rings.

People sitting in front of my desk generally feel about the way they do at the dentist's. They show up because they are in some kind of trouble and this represents a last resort. Sometimes charm helps, sometimes not; this time I didn't know, so I let it be.

"How can I help you, Ms. Stewart?" I asked.

She told me she was a caseworker and job counselor with the state's Department of Social Services. For the past three years she had been working mostly with Lowell's Southeast Asian population, which, after that of Long Beach, California, included the largest group of Cambodians in the U.S.

"Two weeks ago, on June twenty-seventh," she said, "a man was murdered here. Do you remember it?"

I might not have if *she* hadn't been doing the asking. The only real estate market not in a slump was graveyard plots. "Cambodian, wasn't he?"

"Yes. Bhuntan Tran. I worked with him when he first

5

arrived. He was already educated, but I got him into English classes at the junior college. He held down two jobs."

"Ambitious."

"He was an inspiration to a lot of others in the community."

"His house was in Belvidere, as I recall," I said. It was the high-rent end of town.

"A small one on Longfellow Street. Paid for with a lot of hard work and sweat and owned by the bank just like everyone else's." Her eyes sparked and two spots of rose came to her matte-finish cheeks. "Mr. Rasmussen, why is it with so many 'Americans' "—she supplied the quotes with her tone—"that while getting ahead is what they live for, when they see a well-dressed Hispanic woman, or a black man driving a Mercedes, it's suddenly unfair."

"Was I implying," I said, "or are you inferring?"

"I don't know you, and I shouldn't judge. It's just that I've seen it so often. It irks me. People want to throw up barricades around the country, and everyone who isn't in can stay the hell out." She stopped, maybe contrite all of a sudden; probably just convinced I was not worth the energy. Her features softened a little, and she looked around. "Could I have a glass of water?"

I got it, pouring it from a plastic gallon jug into a clean mug. "You don't like city water?" she asked.

"This time of the year it tastes like it comes out of the tadpole tank in the fifth-grade science class."

"You should've heard Bhuntan tell about drinking water. In Phnom Penh he was an environmental engineer. He had to bury the fact that he had an education just to stay alive. The Khmer Rouge emptied the entire city and drove everyone out into the country to work like pack animals."

"Grim. I saw *The Killing Fields*," I said.

6

"I'm talking life, not Hollywood. Bhuntan's wife and kids never made it out. He went to a camp in Thailand, and later got to California. When he came here, I helped him get work. He ended up a lab assistant in a plastics plant, and a laundryman at night. Forget the fact that he held a Ph.D."

"Prejudice stinks," I agreed, "but I'm not sure this office is where it gets redressed."

"I guess I'm just tired of seeing America duck out of its promise."

"You won't get an argument from me."

That dulled the last of her attack. She sipped the water, then slid closer in the chair. "The reason I came isn't to beat up on you. I'm concerned with Bhuntan's murder. The truth is I'm frustrated with the police investigation."

"Have you spoken with them?"

"Twice. The second time was yesterday afternoon. I talked with a Sergeant St. Onge."

I knew then where she had got my name. "In person?"

"Yes. He said there were drugs found at Bhuntan's home."

"It was in the paper," I said.

"Well, I don't believe it."

"I don't think the police would make up something like that."

"Cambodians and drugs don't fit together."

"Come on. These days?"

"It's rare."

"Maybe this was the exception."

She shook her head. The movement had the certainty her knock had had. "Then something's wrong somewhere. In fact, Sergeant St. Onge hinted that he had details he hasn't revealed."

"For now, probably. That's standard practice."

7

"I'd like to hire you," she said.

I could have told her the job was strictly a police job. My usual gig was civil investigations, insurance, saving the occasional good name from the breath of scandal. I thought about the photos, which should be going in the mail right then. "I'm not sure this is something for me," I said.

"It isn't your specialty?"

"You could say that."

"I guess I didn't know where else to go."

"If Tran was such a model citizen, what about the Cambodian community?"

"They're newcomers here, most of them. They're not ready to challenge the power too directly."

"But you are?"

"Someone has to."

I sighed. "The police are still the ones who'll handle it best," I said. *Sometimes,* I added to myself. Sage counsel, Rasmussen. Words of wisdom from one who should know.

"Sergeant St. Onge got stern yesterday. I don't think he's eager to talk to me again soon."

I knew what she meant. When they didn't want to give it, getting information from cops was a pick-ax operation. Still, Ed St. Onge was a good cop. He would do his job. I took a sip of coffee. I had the feeling that it meant Ada Stewart's whole sense of herself that Bhuntan Tran not be condemned with having brought on his own death by having got in wrong with drugs. In the fifteen minutes she had been there, I had developed a healthy respect for the woman. A good social worker made what I do look like fooling with Play-Doh. Maybe we needed more concerned ones like her before we all went down the tube.

Still, it didn't stack up for me. Two weeks was not a long

8

time for a police investigation. But I also knew the longer a case went unsolved, the less likely it ever would be. So flip the coin. Heads they win, tails you lose. I said: "All right."

Her eyes widened. "You'll investigate?"

"I'll have a look."

She snapped open the little candy bag. "I can give you some cash, or a check . . ."

"Whichever's easier. It's two and a half for a retainer, which is also the rate per day, plus any out-of-pocket."

"Two and a half—that's two hundred and fifty dollars?" she asked.

I nodded. "If I can't find anything promising in a day, then we should talk and decide if this is worth your spending the money."

"Let's make it two days then. Five hundred dollars."

I liked her math.

"Don't worry about the money," she said, the way everyone said it. I bundled bounced checks for the Cub Scout paper drive.

I opened the desk's lone drawer, took out a business card from the deck of five hundred, crossed out one *s* in my name and inserted it later on with a caret. Printer's error, but I had let it slide; figured I had a favor coming. Lately I had been thinking about asking him to print tens and twenties; but maybe that could wait now. She wrote the check out and handed it across. Ada *Chan* Stewart: hunch confirmed.

"Is this a current phone, Ms. Stewart?"

"Yes, and my office phone's on here." She gave me one of her Massachusetts DSS cards. I gave her a receipt.

"I'll be in touch in a day or two," I said as I walked her through the waiting room to the outer door, "but if you have any questions, feel free to call."

"Thank you."

She was a lot less nervous than when she had come in twenty minutes ago. She paused in the doorway and played her trump smile. "Detective St. Onge was right about you."

Oh, what the hell; everyone else was being a comic this morning. "Is he still gossiping about how brave and handsome I am?"

Ada Chan Stewart's mouth curled, and I almost expected to see her giggle into her hand, but that had been left behind generations ago, on a boat. She just gave a healthy jingle of laughter. "He said you'd be easy to hire."

2

ↄ⋊ⓔⓍⓔⓍⓔⓍⓔⓍⓔↄ

I WALKED ACROSS Kearney Square
to the postal branch and mailed my report, with the figure
studies and good wishes to the congressional aspirant,
then set off on foot down Merrimack.

Lowell's downtown streets had been laid out nearly two
centuries ago. Through a lapse in illogic, Merrimack actually ran parallel to the river of the same name. The building facades were four- and five-story brick with
brownstone flourishes, like buildings in an Edward Hop-
per painting. They were a dusty color now, slashed with
morning sunlight that forgave the sins of blandness. With
broad sidewalks and gold-lettered store signs and early
visitors to the national and state parks, downtown was actually charming in the July warmth. But it was illusory.
There was no anchor here. At night you could sling a
bowling ball down the sidewalks and not hit a soul. The
area became a ghost town except for the restless
motorama of cruising cars. These were the dispossessed—
Hispanic, Portuguese, Indo-Chinese, and working-class
white kids, for whom pride in a home was beyond reach,
and so the big rumbly Detroit iron became both a limit
and a badge of freedom. "I'm somebody," the nobodies
said with their skreeling rubber.

I nodded to a few passersby, said good morning to a few others, but not many. Lowell had grown too big. I was just as glad.

It did feel good to be out though—and walking at midmorning on a Wednesday was another kind of freedom. But thinking about it, Ed St. Onge's quip to Ada Stewart about my availability scurried across my sunshine like a small gray cloud. I was susceptible to cracks from cops because I had been one for eight years, a dick, same as St. Onge.

The police station was in the JFK Civic Center, next door to city hall, around the corner from the public library. The latter two had been built when Benjamin Harrison was president and looked like they would last as long as the New Hampshire hills their granite had been hacked out of. The cop shop was new—slabs of prestressed concrete with glass and aluminum, union-built. I'd give it another ten years.

Up three steps was a brick-paved area and a double row of trees with spiky branches, from which hung curly pods. The trees were locusts, which are about as native to these parts as Buddhists. Someone had figured the trees gave class to city hall plaza, though I'd bet there wasn't a cop or a politician within bribing distance who had the foggiest idea what kind of trees they were.

Inside the lobby I slipped through a glass door behind a pair of women who were arguing with the desk officer in mile-a-minute Spanish. I just waved without making eye contact, hipped through the hinged gate and went back through the reception area. Do it with élan, and the world is your oyster.

I walked down a long corridor where a glass-block halfwall lent light and mystery to offices along one side. There were two other men in the end office with St. Onge, the three of them looking at a computer screen, talking. The two were a pair of plainclothes named Gus Deemys and Roland Cote. When they saw me, their chins quit. Deemys hoisted his trim form off the edge of St. Onge's desk and tugged his suit jacket straight: brown on a beige shirt and green silk tie. He was a dresser. "Catch you, Ed," he told St. Onge.

"Yeah," said Cote. They strolled past, into the corridor.

St. Onge pecked briefly at the computer keyboard, and the data vanished from the screen. He pulled a toothpick from his mouth like he was going to say something, but he didn't, so I did. "I love walking in and seeing a room light up."

He pointed the toothpick at the door. I closed it.

"What do I have to do, Ed? Wave a white flag?"

"Kind of late for that. What happened never should've in the first place," he said. "None of it."

I couldn't deny it, so I didn't. He gave a gruff sigh that was meant to say, What the hell, I'm just a big softie at heart. "Sit."

Ed was in his mid-forties, with a dark moustache and hair fading like a pair of scuffed Navy shoes. He had half-moon crinkles on his cheeks under the eyes. He hauled a deck of Camels from the pocket of his short-sleeve shirt, wandered over to the window that looked out at a Dumpster behind Pollard Memorial Library and lit up. He fanned out the match and sucked smoke. I decided there were more interesting sights than the seat of his pants.

The framed Sierra Club print on the wall behind his desk was new. It showed a mountain meadow confettied

13

with wildflowers. Dealing all the time with the worst that city streets and the human soul could toss at you, you wanted to believe there was peace somewhere. Could be it was a sucker's game though. As soon as you walked into the scene in the poster, any peace thereabouts hightailed it for the hills. As Thoreau said, more or less, peace is where people ain't.

"So what's what?" St. Onge said at last, turning.

I lifted my eyebrows. "Spreading tales about a round-heeled P.I. again?"

He moved smoke around in his mouth like he was deciding whether to do rings or something really fancy. "So she went. She was bound and determined to do something. I figured you wouldn't rip her off at least."

"I appreciate it. I think. Though I'm not sure what I can do."

"She's as persistent as she is cute, I give her that."

"And you wanted quits."

He came over and parked a haunch on the corner of his desk, which was only a little bigger than mine but had a lot more paper on it. He pinched up the knee of one pant leg. There was a slight flare to the cuff, I saw, but on a local cop's salary, it made sense to keep your suits and hope the style rolled around again before they had to bury you in one of them.

"There's nothing to tell her," he said. "You know the routine. The Tran killing's just one of the six we've got ongoing. Don't you read the *Sun*?"

"I stare at the sign all day. That count?"

His expression didn't unsour.

"Yeah," I admitted, "I did read there might be a drug tie-in."

"We found blow at the scene."

"I wondered about that. The paper didn't say how much, either."

"What diff?"

"Ten pounds? Dust on a mirror? Come on, you sent the woman my way, you had to figure I'd come asking."

He drew in smoke so deep I expected to see it come wisping out of his flared cuff. But it didn't come out anywhere for a full minute, during which he leaned across his desk and carefully stubbed the butt into a tray of bent friends. When the smoke did appear, there were words in it.

"Half a gram. In a little plastic film canister, with Tran's prints on it. I know, it could've been just a recreational honk."

"Or planted," I said.

"Or it could very definitely be tied in. People get iced for pocket lint, dammit." He climbed off the desk.

"Touchy," I said.

He went to the window again.

"You implied to Ada Chan Stewart that you're sitting on evidence."

He began to whistle through his teeth.

"Any hints?" I said.

The tune could have been "I've Been Working on the Railroad."

"Got a weapon?" I said.

On second thought it was "Good Night, Ladies."

"Come on, don't I always let you stand in a circle and clap when I do my fancy stuff at the policeman's ball?" I said.

"Not this time, Raz."

"That bus runs two ways. Think about it."

Maybe he did. Maybe he admitted to himself that having a private cop who played straight with him had occasional advantages. He checked the shine on one shoe and buffed it on the back of a trouser leg. When he had brought the other shoe up to luster, he turned. "This is between us."

"Okay."

"If a person who shall remain nameless found out I'd leaked investigative info, he'd have me raking the pods from those damn trees out front, whatever the hell they are."

"Locusts," I said. "Forewarned."

"We're working the angle this one could've been a professional hit," he said. "It has the looks."

That woke me up a little. It also made me wary. Nothing takes heat off a killing—and therefore the police—like calling it gangland. Folks figure, Hey, play with fire you get burnt, victim probably got his due. Pros aren't interested in plain old tax-paying me.

St. Onge said, "Tran was shot twice in the back of the head. Twenty-two pistol, point-blank range."

I gave a low whistle, no tune at all. "Suspects?"

"Nope, and if it's tied to drugs, I'm not sure we'll find one."

"If not?"

"Find a suspect?"

"If not tied to drugs."

He picked up his Camels. I saw they were Lights—the reports had scared him *that* much anyway. He tapped one out and got it burning. "It sounded to me like Miss Stewart is looking to keep this Tran as a model to the community. If he *was* straight—though I'm betting against." He shrugged. "I don't know."

"And I do?"

16

"You don't have the same cuffs on you I've got."

I smiled, I couldn't help it. He frowned and kept talking. "Most of these people are okay, from what I can tell. Except for the little turds in the gangs. But the others work hard and keep their noses clean. Let's face it, though: they see cops come around with a lot of questions, they've got to have some hairy flashbacks, some of them. We've already run into trouble just trying to get them to talk to us."

"Maybe you need some new icebreakers."

"They think we're there to hassle them, they hide. Someone with a lower profile . . . they might open up a little."

"You're looking for a coal-mine canary."

He gave a smoky grin that put little down-turned smiles under his eyes. "I'm just saying you and I might help each other out."

"Old time's sake?" I said. Still, he was right in one sense. Cop work these days is all paper. Someone had estimated that taking one bad guy off the streets costs sixty trees. Being private gave me a mobility he didn't have. But, for resources, I had only my shoes and two days' pay.

"I'm not taking her money if there's no place to go."

"Not saying you should."

"I told her a day or two."

"So it takes three. She wants to know. It isn't going to break her bank."

"I don't work for free," I said.

He gave a skeptical snort. "She's good for it."

"You know that?"

"You did recognize the name, didn't you, Sherlock?"

"She related to Charlie Chan?"

"Her great-grandfather was Charles Blaine Stewart."

I hadn't even been close. So when she had said not to

worry about the money, she was telling the truth. Charles Blaine Stewart had been in the clipper ship trade to China when they still called it the Opening of the Orient. The estate he had left filled a museum and about twenty prime acres in Andover, two towns east. I wondered if one of Ada's forebears had been a little China doll that the old man had collected and brought back with him.

"Do I get to eyeball your report?" I asked.

"Of course not."

"I'd like to hand her the execution angle at least. She's tuned in to the community, maybe she's heard something."

That he could allow. I jotted down a few details. This would be more interesting than walking around the Raytheon buildings punching tape. And maybe I could give Ada Chan Stewart a truer picture of Bhuntan Tran's last days, whatever it turned out to be. I had a feeling she would accept only the truth.

"So, business done," he said. "You hear from Lauren?"

"Ask me tomorrow. We're having dinner tonight."

He gauged me a moment. "Good luck."

As I headed for the door, he called for me to stop. I knew why. The bullhorn voice that had started up in the corridor outside was one I knew too well. Lieutenant Francis X. Droney was giving somebody the big chew. The chewee made some reply, but it was like the cry of a mole under a rotary mower. The glass block wall gave their shapes a staircase effect, like figures embroidered in a country sampler, but the language was city stuff all the way. After a moment the figures moved off in opposite directions and Droney's voice was silenced by a slamming door.

St. Onge ground another butt into his ashtray.

"Figured neither of us wanted you to walk into the Ogre."

He figured right. Down the hall, and even after I got outside among the locusts, I kept trying to think of someone I would want to see less. A dentist telling me I had six months of gum work ahead came close, but Droney still won out.

3

꧁꧂꧁꧂꧁꧂

THAT TV STUFF about bullet-riddled car chases is bunk, and with my eight-year-old steel-gray Bobcat, it was going to stay that way. My wants were simple: leg room for the six-one stretch and space overhead for thinking. I also required a heater that throws flames on a bitter January night when I'm watching a drawn shade on a street so lonely even the rats are blue. With me, wheels were a matter of cost and visibility: I wanted it low on both counts. Back in the alley behind my office I fired up and got wheeling east on Merrimack, the tattoo of knocks from the engine beating light rhythm to my thoughts.

Belvidere is one long ridge sloping away on all sides, making snobbery an exact science. On top are the castles that the mill owners and captains of industry built a century ago, and which would not be ashamed to rear their turreted heights in Newport. On the downslope toward the heart of the city, the houses are still big, but as elevation declines, so do values. At the bottom, butting the Concord River, you got so much vinyl siding in pastel shades you could be in East Boston.

The Tewksbury side of the hill, rolling away from downtown, has little neighborhoods of bungalows and capes, mostly well-kept and tucked behind hedgerows. I had to check my street map for Longfellow. Logic would have put it somewhere near Emerson and Hawthorne, but that would have made sense. I found it off Butman, nary a blacksmith or spreading chestnut tree in sight.

Even without a P.I. ticket, I would have had an easy go of finding the house. A kid in a pale blue shirt with loops of perspiration darkening the underarms was hammering a Century 21 realtor's stake into the small front lawn. As I got out, a neighbor from the adjacent house looked up from hosing his lawn and gave me a hostile stare. The kid with the sledgehammer paused to swipe a forearm across his brow, nodded my way, and went back to pounding. With a stroke like that he'd never want for work in Transylvania. Around here, though, with the real estate market softer than a Republican's wallet, it was a dubious skill.

"Nice morning for it," I said.

"Hi there. It is."

He was a beefy, freckled kid, his rosy cheeks as wet as the ink probably was on his broker's license. He took a last whack, then stopped to catch his breath and test the post for rigidity. He seemed satisfied. "Want to buy it?" he said hopefully. "This is an established neighborhood."

"I guess that explains the guy with the hose."

"*Him.* He says to me when I came today—no good morning, or nothing—he says, 'I hope you're gonna be careful who you sell that to.' " The kid shook his head and laughed wonderingly.

He said his name was Ken Smith. He handed me the sledgehammer while he dug out his card. I liked his hard sell. If he were a dog, he'd be panting in the kitchen as you asked your mom if you could keep him. I told him who I was and asked if I could look around. He didn't see why not.

"It'll give me a chance to check it out again. We just got

the listing and haven't done a caravan yet. The bank bought it from the estate. I used to get a funny twinge about a house that came on the market on account of a divorce, back when I first started in real estate." Back in his apprenticeship days no doubt, a hoary six months before. "But this . . . it's kinda sad."

I agreed. "Do you know who inherited the estate?"

"No. Sorry."

We went up the driveway. The house was a gray Cape Cod with an unattached garage, no car inside. From the porch I peered into a small back yard in need of a mow. There was an old antenna clothesline pitched in a sunny corner back there with a few clothespins still clamped in place, like anorexic sparrows on a telephone wire. Beyond that grew a thicket of swamp maples. Ken Smith jingled an impressive clump of keys and got us in.

The kitchen was tidy, with a linoleum floor fashioned to look like tiny bricks, cherry veneer cabinets, and white curtains edged with blue gingham. On a small table sat an optimistic pile of listing sheets. Ken Smith's blazer hung on the back of a chair in a color that looked best squiggled on hotdogs.

I picked up an info sheet and set the sledgehammer on the rest. I studied the details briefly, noting numbers and a name, then we strolled through the house together. Ken Smith pointed out features while I mulled the layout with another purpose in mind. I wanted to know what had happened here on a Tuesday night two weeks ago.

The house had the staple cape layout: kitchen, living room, two bedrooms, bath, with concealed stairs in the center leading to a basement and to an unfinished attic.

"The bedroom carpeting is new," Ken Smith said, "in case you're wondering."

I hadn't been. Only on TV do people get shot to death without it making a mess. The little house fairly sparkled. The victim had been found in the back bedroom. The wallpaper there had been washed, but I could make out the ghost shapes of stains below a window that faced to the side. I bent and peered through the gap under the drawn shade and the top of the Sears air conditioner. The adjacent house was twenty feet away, beyond a six-foot Cyclone fence woven with green and white plastic strips. Beyond it I saw the blue-green shimmer of a swimming pool. The other window in the bedroom faced the back yard, which ran sixty feet to woods that backed all the small yards on this side of Longfellow.

The second bedroom, in front of the kitchen, was decorated as a kids' room, probably left over from whoever had owned the house before Tran. The wallpaper depicted *Sesame Street* characters, and I realized that had Tran's children survived the monster with the jolly name of Pol Pot, they would have known Oscar and Big Bird. I looked in the cellar, then poked my head into the attic. In the kitchen Ken Smith pulled on his blazer. He used one of his keys to lock up and we walked outside together.

"Did you find any clues?" he asked.

"The police do a pretty good job with that. I'd guess they found whatever there was to find."

"But no killer yet, huh?"

"Not yet."

"I hope they do. Or you do. Really."

From the lawn, he gazed back at the house: fading shingles with green shutters in which shamrocks had been cut with a scroll saw. The asphalt roof had a few winters left in it, though the ceramic cat was a question mark. Ken

23

Smith's freckled brow ridged, his enthusiasm sagging for a second. "I hope it isn't gonna be a jinx."

"It'll sell. People forget. It's a tidy little house." And it was.

"Sure," he agreed, confident again. "It's a great starter."

"In an established neighborhood," I reminded him. We shook hands and I thanked him for his time.

"Hey, in this business you got nothing but. Can I ask you one thing, though?" He nodded at the Bobcat. "You being a P.I. and all—is that really your car?"

"It's a loaner," I said. "Even as we speak, the Lamborghini's in the shop getting bullet holes patched."

A grin plumped his bright cheeks.

"My turn now," I said. "I can see you wear the uniform with pride. Do you own the sport coat, or do they?"

He laughed. I gunned him with a finger pistol and headed for the street. He'd do okay. The house would be a slow sell any way you sliced it—which was why they had given it to him. But they'd leave the *l* out and settle for "homey" in the ad, and a couple or a young family would pick it up and life would go on. I wished them all well.

The neighbor with the hose had worked his way to the far end of his property, and I strolled down to where he was. He had a jar attachment on the hose and was spraying a fourth-generation Agent Orange on a clump of toadstools that had pitched camp on his lawn.

"Nice morning for it," I said. I like to stay with a snappy opener.

He looked as if he'd have liked to hose me down and watch me wither. "Who're you?"

He was in Madras walk shorts and a V-necked T-shirt. He was probably little more than my age—give him two

24

and make it forty—but he had the Budweiser gut and could ask Santa for a training bra any time now. I went through my half of the introductions and got nothing in return. I might have hung it up right there, but it's the shark-infested eyes that see things. "I'd like to ask a few questions," I said.

"I don't see some ID, I'm gonna call someone who will."

The wallet copy of my private license earned a prolonged stare and finally a grunt. "I already talked to the cops. They given up?"

"I'm cooperating with them. I won't keep you, Mr. . . ?"

He was slow about it. "Azar."

"I noticed the bedroom window over there faces your house and pool."

"Yeah?"

"Any chance you saw or heard something the night of the shooting?"

"Wasn't home."

He was a fun type. But it didn't figure he had all that swimming pool alone. Judging from his physique, it didn't figure he had it at all. "What about your family?"

He strangled off the hose and walked back to a green metal reel at the spigot. I followed him. There was a black Bronco in the driveway, tinted glass, Yosemite Sam snarling "Back Off" from the mudflaps.

"Family?" I repeated.

Azar grunted. "No one heard nothing."

I saw it move across his face like a shadow, and I didn't want it to get away. "Any theories?"

He hesitated, then scowled. "I don't think the cops've gotta look far to figure who did it."

"Yeah?" My interest stayed with him.

25

"This is a regular neighborhood. You won't find many of the *other* people."

He gave the adjective a nasty little emphasis, and there it was. "I got nothing against anyone minds their own business," he went on, "but people should stick to their own kind. And I don't like wild parties till all hours, I can tell you that."

"Bhuntan Tran had parties?"

"Tell the truth, Joe," a woman's voice said through a screen window above a hemlock bush. A face to go with it leaned forward on the sill. "I'm Claire Azar. Are you from the police?"

"Private," I told her. "My name's Rasmussen."

She glanced sidelong, indicating the house next door. "There was one party. Actually, more of a cookout, wouldn't you say, Joe?"

Joe stewed, but Claire took no notice. "Mr. Tran came over very polite and shy the day before and asked me if we'd like to come. It was some sort of Cambodian celebration, back in May. I'd like to have gone. Learning about other cultures is an education in itself. I love the *Geographic* specials. But we were going up to Hampton to visit Joe's side that day. We didn't get back till late. They were a little lively over there, it's true. But mostly it was just talking, which if it'd been English, we wouldn't even have noticed. And everyone was gone by midnight."

Azar looked sullenly at his wife. "You going to tell the rest?"

"Moon festival," she said abruptly.

"I'm sorry?" I said.

"What the celebration was for. In May. I just remembered it."

"What did you mean by 'the rest'?" I asked Azar.

He was still looking at his wife. "Well?"

Claire Azar left the window and came out the front door and down the steps, rubber thongs clapping softly against her bare heels. She was a tanned, fit woman wearing pink culottes and a tank top. I knew who used the pool in back.

"The night before the awful thing happened," she said, "I was home. Joe works three to eleven. So I was here alone, watching TV on the breezeway. *Murphy Brown* I think I was watching. Anyway, during a commercial I got up, and suddenly I thought I saw someone in the back yard. I peered through the blinds and sure enough, someone had come out of the woods behind Mr. Tran's house. That's all woods back there, runs over to Brae Road. Kids play in it sometimes, but it's swampy and this time of year it's all mosquitoes. Anyway, I see someone I think is a kid, and he jogs across the lawn and I guess went to the back porch on the far side."

"Of Tran's house?" I asked.

"That's a guess, because I only saw him go around the side and then I didn't see him again."

"Did you recognize the kid?"

"Well, that's the thing. I don't think it was a kid. I mean, he was slender, but I think it was a man."

"That was the night before the killing?" I said.

"Right. Monday. The next night I fell asleep early. Some neighbors down the street say they heard a car leave around eleven, but nobody saw anything."

That had been in St. Onge's version. "Do you remember anything else about the person you saw?"

She scratched her tanned elbow a moment. "Did I mention that he was Oriental?"

* * *

27

I asked a few more questions, but there wasn't much else to be learned. As I walked to my car, Azar stood at the edge of his lawn, treating me the whole time to his bunker stare like I was going to sneak around some night while he was at work and mix it up with Claire and maybe queer Century 21's deal in the bargain and then no nice regular people would ever move into the house next door. It would be haunted with slant-eyed ghosts, and toadstools would invade the back yard, and kids would throw rocks through the windows on Halloween. That's how it starts, his bitter eyes told me as I turned the car around and drove away.

There was no street sign on Brae Road. Probably in some college dorm room in Boston. The street was one closer to the hill, so the homes were larger, all-American ranches and splits. School vacation was less than a month old and the kids were sitting among their bikes, skateboard ramps and street hockey nets, staring and idle-minded. These established neighborhoods were starting to get to me.

I was interested in one stretch of road where there were no houses, only a sandy shoulder alongside woods that came out on the back yards of the homes on Longfellow. The woods was a tangle of green gloom in the July midday, and I could imagine someone pulling over that Monday night and parking to slip guerrilla-like through the two hundred feet of trees and swamp. One of the "other people," in Azar's crude-but-true parlance. I drove off with a cool sense of how little I knew of my Southeast Asian townsmen.

4

❦❦❦❦❦❦❦

WITH PLANS FOR dinner at six, I de-
cided to pass on lunch. I found a phone booth and called
the *Sun* and asked for Bob Whitaker. He had just come out
of the darkroom. We kibitzed for a minute, then I told him
I needed a favor. He didn't go "Uh oh" or anything, so I
mentioned the Tran killing. "I want to know if there've
been other murders of Southeast Asians in the past year,
Cambodians in particular."

"In Lowell?"

"Anywhere in the country."

"Do you want it before Christmas?"

It was a tall order, especially since Bob was a photographer. It would mean combing the *Sun's* files; but he had
the best access of anyone I was friends with. "Sooner the
better."

He said he would get back. I dropped more coin and
called the company where Bhuntan Tran had been employed days. A woman with a voice that would never be
replaced by a robot said, "TecStrand." I told her who I
was and that I wanted to talk with Bhuntan Tran's supervisor, and without having said a second word she put me
through. I got sandbagged at the next level and told the
plant was in a production cycle—I would have to make an
appointment for next week sometime.

"That'd be great," I said. "No problem. The thing is I'll be in Washington all next week, appearing before the Senate Committee on Law and Order."

"Minute please." The person was gone for a few bars of "Yellow Bird," then came back. "Would tomorrow morning at ten be convenient?"

"Um . . ." My calendar was as bare as the Playmate of the Month, but once you start the tangled web, you have to keep weaving. I rattled pages of the phone book. "I can just make that."

"I've put you in, sir. Mr. Turcotte, ten A.M."

The laundry was easy. Shifts changed at three-thirty, come by then, ask for Mr. Perry; they'd tell him someone was coming. I cradled the phone and thought about going for four in a row, but I had a pair of hours to kill. Besides, I'm much more impressive in person. I took 113 along the river.

The Merrimack River springs out of mountains up toward the Canadian border, making its debut near Lake Winnipesaukee in New Hampshire, then for a hundred miles keeps dubious company with tired mill cities like Manchester, Nashua, Lowell, Lawrence, and Haverhill before dragging its soiled skirts to the ocean at Plum Island, like an old tart on seaside holiday. But the river made these cities. As it snakes through what is now Lowell, it drops thirty vertical feet, and some smart cookies a long time ago decided to carve the farmland into canals and locks and put all that energy to use. The river is still impressive as it rolls along, particularly on fine days like today when the wind was right and you didn't catch a whiff of it.

In Tyngsborough I went out 3-A. River View Mortgage was housed in a pale-gray-and-blue, gambrel-roof reproduction in rough-sawn clapboard with quaint farm implements over an ersatz barn door. The place fairly oozed down-homeyness—until you couldn't make your monthly payment, then they came at your credit rating with a scythe. I greeted a young woman at a desk inside and asked for R. Morrisette, the name I had taken off the listing sheet Ken Smith had shown me. I was told that Rachel had left the organization.

"Can *I* help you?" the young woman offered. "I'm pretty new, but I try hard." A small diamond solitaire twinkled from her finger, as bright as her personality. I told her who and what I was and didn't get any further. "An honest-to-God detective?" she said.

I could have let her feel the biceps, but that meant taking off my suit jacket and probably popping some shirt seams, so I showed her the license instead.

"We prefer 'investigator' over 'detective,' " I said. "The cops do too."

When she caught her breath, I gave her the mortgage number I was interested in. She left her desk for a few moments and came back with a file folder. A look of pain had come over her face.

"I thought the name was familiar. That's really too bad what happened." The sympathy was genuine. "He was right up-to-date too. Eight hundred fifty-six dollars a month, including twenty-six for mortgage insurance. That was required because he'd put down ten percent."

I counted some mental fingers and toes. "So last February Mr. Tran fronted about seventeen thousand dollars for the house, give or take."

"Plus a point and a half and whatever the lawyers held him up for. And after all that . . . *tch.* Imagine."

I was thinking of Ada Chan Stewart's remark about

31

saving. It was a hefty nut to make on laundry money. "Who holds the note now?"

"Central West Mortgage. Secondary market."

As I was wondering where to go, she said in a confidential voice, "Mr. Tran also included a gift letter with his loan ap."

"Refresh my memory."

"A gift letter? Anytime you have money that's been given to you, the mortgagor requires a letter from the giver, stating it was a gift, free and clear. So it doesn't represent a liability. Mr. Tran got five thousand dollars from . . . a cousin, it says."

"The cousin have a name?"

"Suo— . . ." She frowned into the file a moment, then grinned and gave it a quarter turn. "I'm not even going to try that one."

The name typed on the line was Suoheang Khoy. I didn't try it either, but I wrote it down. The address was a P.O. box in San Jose, California. The rest of the file was routine lawyer fodder. I wondered how many trees it cost to buy a house.

The young woman had been helpful, so I thanked her and gave her a card with the *s* inked into the right spot. I didn't think she would be needing it anytime soon, but like the song said, a diamond doesn't always sparkle. I hoped hers would. If nothing else, she could keep the card in her wallet and write other people's phone numbers on the back.

The Ajax Linen Company's logo—a helmeted spear-carrier—was painted in faded lines on a brick wall facing an alley where I parked.

The three-thirty shift was in full hiss and roar; I could

feel the crease dissolving from my pants as soon as I stepped inside the building. A lot of people were trundling big canvas hampers around in the sultry air, fitting sheets and pillow cases on industrial pressers. I asked a towering black man where I could find Mr. Perry. He nodded toward a glass door at the far end.

The office was a snug little affair with a rolltop desk. Years of steam had not even started to warp the slab oak. A bearded man with long hair stood in a corner plucking punch cards out of a rack under a time clock.

"I'm looking for Mr. Perry," I said.

He turned and regarded me with sharp eyes. He had a potato nose with pores in it as big as the eyelets on his work boots. His uniform was a tie-dyed tank top and jeans held aloft by a garrison belt with a ZigZag man buckle, his wallet secured to the belt with the *Queen Mary's* anchor chain. He gave a grunt that could have meant most anything.

"Is that you?" I asked.

"There ain't no 'mister.' It's Perry *Martin*. Who the hell are you?"

I knew my earlier message had been like a penny foolishly tossed down a wishing well. I went through the explanation; it's amazing how often you need to when you're working, but it beat the silence of not working all hollow. Perry Martin checked time cards and made little jottings on each, one furry shoulder turned to me as he talked, all to the only slightly muted accompaniment of the anvil chorus outside the door. Tran got a good rating as a worker.

"Did he use drugs?" I asked.

Martin's eyes locked with mine, lots of challenge and who knew what else in them. "What're you, a narc? I wouldn't have cared if he was into sniffing *toilet* seats in his spare time. If I had a dozen of him, I'd get ridda the wetbacks and bushboogies who want a paycheck but don't wanna earn it."

"Is that a yes?" I asked.

Just then there was a knock, and a black woman carrying a flower print carpetbag opened the door and hurried in.

" 'Scuse me," she murmured and went to the punch clock before she saw the cards were gone. She looked over. "Sorry, Perry," she said. "My little girl's sick and I had to wait on my husband to get home from his shift to be with her. I'd rather run a little late here and make the time up by staying longer."

Perry had been looking over, nodding in what might have been sympathy. "Daughter sick, huh, Cassie?"

"I'll make up the time." She was dressed in a loose polyester dress, a big woman with a strong, handsome face and expressive eyes. "Nervous" was stamped in those eyes now. Her hands worried at the handle of her carpetbag. "I can stay extra."

"Extra? Naw," Perry said. "Tell you what. Why don't you take the week off and come back Monday."

"Mr. Martin, you can't *do* that."

"I just done it. I ain't taking any of that *late* news. People got a shift to work, I expect them punching in when they're supposed to."

The woman stood a moment and I tried to study the wall. Humiliation in the face of white males probably was nothing new to her, but it hurt me. From the outer area, over the silence, came the rumble of laundry machinery. At last, in a weak voice, the woman said, "Monday?"

"On time," Perry said.

34

She turned and went slowly out and pulled the door closed behind her.

"Kind of a tough policy," I said.

He gave me the stone stare. "I tell you how to do your job?"

I stared back. After a moment he twitched his mouth and turned to the desk. "That's why Tran was a pain in the ass," he said. "He'd fight me now to get her reinstated. I'd still make the call. I've got a business to run. But he worked hard, I'll give the little son of a bitch that. And, no, I don't think he was a doper."

Driving out I noticed the woman who had been inside. She stood across the street waiting for a city bus. I stopped. "I'm going downtown if that's any help."

She checked me warily, looked to see no bus in sight, then picked up her parcel. "Gorham Street's where I'm headed if you're going that far."

"It's on the way."

The silence sat around us in a sluggish pool most of the way down Lawrence Avenue and I began to think I should have kept right on driving and not stopped. There was no way to acknowledge what had just occurred. Instead I said, "Did you know Bhuntan Tran very well?"

"You a policeman?"

"No. Tran was a friend of a friend."

She nodded. "He had no trouble making them."

"Why's that?"

"Folks took to Bhuntan, because he took to folks. Always smiling and talking. That was real sad what happened."

"Did Bhuntan seem different at all when you saw him last?"

"Different? Well, now that you mention it, the day

35

before he got killed, he come in and asked Perry for the second half of his shift off. That wasn't like him."

"How do you mean?"

"I mean, Bhuntan was a *worker*."

"Do you know why he asked to leave?"

"He didn't say, but if I was to guess? I'd say there was something he had to do, something he didn't much want to do."

I glanced over at her.

"His face," she said. "He looked scared."

I negotiated past several double-parked cars to a four-way stop. Shifts had ended and the liquor store on one corner was doing brisk business, like the bar on the opposite corner. "Scared," I said when we were rolling again.

"Looked it to me. He wasn't his usual self. Seemed kind of uptight." She ventured a tart smile. "The way I must've looked back there in the office a while ago."

"You handled it about the best way there was, Mrs. . . . ?"

"It's Samms, but make it Cassie."

"Thanks. Mine's Rasmussen. Alex."

"I'd have liked to tell the man what for, but I need the job."

"I know the feeling."

"The truth is it was my second late this week, which makes only two times ever. Generally my daughter's tough as weeds, but the other week she went swimming and took an ear infection, so she's home. I figure she needs me more for those few minutes than some company's sheets and table linen do."

I nodded. "Mrs. Samms—Cassie—did Tran ever show any signs of drug use?"

"Back to Bhuntan again, huh?"

36

"Off the record," I said, "I'm a private investigator. The person who hired me doesn't think Tran used drugs."

"*Him?* Shoot, who the police kidding on that one? He was straight up. Put your mind to ease on that."

I sneaked through a yellow light, went past the old Boston and Maine depot and drew to a stop in front of the defunct Rialto theater. Cassie Samms opened the door. I said, "Are you looking for another job?"

Some of the wariness sparked in her eyes again. "Kind of job?"

"I can't promise anything, but the assistant manager over at the Appleton Inn is a friend. She hires the staff. Would you consider talking to her?"

The idea seemed to interest her.

"Call there and ask for Nan Crawford."

On the curb, she thanked me for the ride and the job tip.

"Use my name," I said. "Then watch out for the doors swinging magically open."

The office was in a lull, but the day's mail told me I was a winner in a seven-figure sweepstakes. I didn't call my broker. There was an offer to time-share in Mexico and a lingerie catalog addressed to a former tenant. I telephoned Ada Chan Stewart's work number. An earnest young woman told me she was out visiting one of her clients but would be back later for a staff meeting. I left word that I would be in touch in the morning.

I got a blank folder out of the top drawer of the file cabinet, reeled a strip of labels into the Royal, typed Ada Stewart's name and affixed the label to the folder. Next I jotted notes on my conversations with the real estate agent, Ken Smith; the Azars; the young woman at River

37

View Mortgage; and Perry Martin from the laundry. I left Cassie Samms's observations to run around in my head for a bit. And while I thought of it, I called the Appleton Inn and got hold of Nan Crawford and told her Mrs. Samms might call. Nan was her usual spry self; in spite of the million and one details of inn-keeping, she made you feel that she had been sitting there all day hoping you would call. When I hung up I re-read the case file.

All of that accomplished, I creaked back in my chair, beached on the downward slope of the afternoon, nothing else to do. Or nothing else I could think of to fill the time. I cranked up Joltin' Joe and brewed a cup of same. The first mouthful hit my stomach and I decided I was jittery enough already.

I used the hallway washroom I shared with Fred Meecham, an attorney who rented a pair of suites down the hall. I wet-combed my hair and poked a fresh dimple into the blue silk foulard, then told the man in the mirror he was out of excuses for stalling.

5

◎◎◎◎◎◎◎◎◎

IT HAD BEEN two months since I had seen Lauren. Possibly I had started to get used to the idea, though I wouldn't press it. Then, two nights before, she was on the phone. She wanted to see me. Dinner Tuesday night? It felt funny making a date with your wife. She picked the place, so I figured the choice of weapons was mine. I had splashed on some Tuscany and worn my gray suit. There wasn't much to be done about the face.

The 99 was a notch above the plastic-roof joints, with okay food and atmosphere if you caught it when the place wasn't packed with the office crowd. I was early. I'm always early. As bad habits go, it's not the worst. A private ticket without a little paranoia doesn't last. I parked on a corner stool at the bar where I could see the door. The bartendress was thirty-something, with a smile full of shiny wire. I told her a Molson. It used to be you would see dental hardware only on kids; these days it turned up everywhere. The soul finally having proven imperfectable, we concentrated on the body now. I had news for us.

Being early was a mistake this time, as it only gave me a chance to worry about what changes two months might have brought. It was more than a year since Lauren had started to tell me we should split. When my counterproposal began to sound like a recording, I said why didn't she stay in the house; it would be easier for me to crash at my office for a while. But as the nights passed, the couch in my waiting room wasn't getting any softer, and the recording only got scratchy from use. Ten months ago I bit the rent on an apartment over in the east end of town. I didn't quit trying to change Lauren's mind.

"Drinking alone?"

I had missed her coming in. I didn't miss anything else as I bumbled to my feet and took in the newly crimped ash-blond hair, her tan, and the trimness the flower-print Belle France dress could only emphasize. As I bent to kiss her she tipped her face just enough so it caught her on the pert angle of her jaw. Charles of the Ritz hit me like a truck pulling out of Memory Lane.

"How are you, Aiex? You look okay."

"Not as okay as you."

She had not put her slim little purse on the bar yet and was taking me in with momentary appraisal in her cool, woodsmoke gray eyes.

"Shall we get a table?" I said.

"Yes," she said. "I'm starved."

I was still feasting on this woman who for a lot of years had been my wife, when a busboy poured water clinking into goblets and asked if we'd care for a cocktail. I looked at Lauren. "Chablis?"

"Cutty and soda," she told him, and in just the way she said it my stomach went tight and my appetite dwindled. I ordered another beer.

There were things you knew about people, the little dance steps you fell into with them which got comfortable. When one or the other partner changed steps, suddenly there were dislocations all down the line. Scotch was a new step.

The early-evening light coming through the latticed window illuminated half of Lauren's face. She wore thirty-eight well, like a suit of custom-fit clothes. She sparkled the way lots of women years younger couldn't, the way, in my eyes, she always had and always would. But something had changed. I sensed it.

After the drinks came and the waiter took our orders, filling his own young eyes with the way Lauren looked, we did the ritual with the glasses, but they were out of key. Lauren snapped open the little purse and found a deck of those women's cigarettes that are as long as an eye pencil, and fitted one in her lips. Clumsily I scratched a restaurant match.

"The rest of the population is giving up and you start?"

She whiffed smoke to one side. "The habit is under control. I end up throwing away half the pack each week because they go stale." Not that it was any of my business, she added without saying it.

I kept it light and we played a little catch-up. Life, work, the mutual and separate friends, the neighborhood. I remembered and told her happy birthday, which was coming up. That struck a spark. She offered her tanned, slender fingers. "You didn't see my birthstone ring."

It was hard to miss a ruby the size of a tail light, but I had. Shamus Rasmussen. "It's great," I said.

The food came and Lauren went at it with zest while I picked at mine like a parakeet. I knew now what I had been hoping for from this, and I'd been wrong. Being wrong makes me defensive, which turns up my smart-ass setting. "Your name gets linked with a certain dry cleaning magnate's lately," I said. "Is that a habit you've got under control too?"

Her eyes went a little stony. "Are you working?"

"Personal curiosity."

41

"You can ask, but I don't have to answer."

I attempted a smile. "We're in an old episode of *Family Feud*, right? Richard Dawson is going to walk in any minute, all puckered up for a kiss."

Her headshake told me I was being childish. I gnawed food and didn't taste a thing. "I don't hear your name on the grapevine," Lauren said neutrally. "Are you seeing anyone?"

"I'm married."

She lifted her shoulders. "That could be a problem. You're thinner."

"The running. Thin is always in."

"Don't get too thin."

"Is that concern I detect?"

"Guilt maybe. Over bailing out the way I did," she said, and for a moment we had slipped into honesty. "My timing wasn't so great. I know that."

I gave her a few seconds to squeeze in more, but she didn't. She stubbed the cigarette into the glass ashtray, where it looked oddly forlorn, alone in the tray with a delicate rim of lipstick on one end. Nothing from lips that pretty should die alone. I leaned closer. "The door swings back the other way," I said, hearing the note of hope in my voice and not ashamed of it.

"That's why I called you," she said.

I felt my heart lift.

"I wanted you to find out first from me," she said, "not around town or in a gossip column. Joel has asked me to marry him, Alex. I want the divorce."

It was like fingers speared into the solar plexus. It is the most helpless feeling there is: you lie there buckled over, fish-eyed and gasping, waiting for the finishing blow.

Lauren looked around, and the waiter glided over. "Same, please," she said. The kid nodded and glanced my

42

way. Seeing the green tinge maybe, he vanished before I could shake my head.

"Why didn't you just order a Molotov and throw that?" I said.

She gazed out at the sparse traffic on 133, and the sunlight loved her face, like the waiter did, like I did, like Joel Castle must. "What did you expect, Alex?" she asked, turning back.

"Time?"

"Dammit, time ran out. I was ready for both of us to leave here, to go someplace new and start over. You insisted on staying."

"There is no place new in a situation like that."

"Isn't there a point where you put your cards down and just walk away, regardless of what's on the table?"

"Not when it's your name that's being dragged through the ashes," I said.

She sighed. "So I'll always admire you for sticking and trying to clear it. But maybe you should've done it another way, not sitting around in a little office with dust motes spinning in the air and waiting for business to find its way up the stairs. You got shafted, that's the way it is. *Every*one gets shafted sooner or later. You pull the shaft out and get the bleeding stopped and you go on. I was ready to do that if we went someplace else. You think it was any easier for *me* reading what the papers were saying about you, knowing what people were thinking? The 'for worse' and 'for poorer' clauses work all right in the beginning, but there's got to be an upward curve."

"Like in the dry cleaning business," I said, being stupid again.

"Like in life. And what's wrong with having money? What have you got against Joel anyway?"

"I know him."

"And I don't?"

"You know his cleaned-up incarnation. I knew him before, when he was Joey Costello, spending his old man's dough and not being a very good person. But that's not—"

"So I accept who he is now. Love can change people."

"Love is just a four-letter word," I said. "Like 'rich.' "

As a credit to her intelligence she sipped her drink and ignored that. But I couldn't. I said, "Okay, he's got good taste, but it doesn't work for Charlie Tuna, why should it work for him? Just because he gives you things and has money, doesn't make it right."

"It's righter than you sitting around feeling sorry for yourself. What's pride worth?"

"If you gotta ask . . ."

She shook her head, truly pained. "Honest to God. I don't know you anymore. What about respect? That's the trouble with you, you respect nothing but some abstraction, some idea of honor that's been wronged."

"Forget about that," I said. "What happened to the couple who were going to stand by each other?" I had taken her hand in mine, but she drew it away, not roughly or abruptly, just away.

"They changed, Alex. People do. Think about that."

She opened her bag, tossed the cigarettes in, took out a wallet and laid some bills on the table. I waved the money away. "Lauren, what if we—"

She cut me off by rising. "I have to leave," she said and hurried for the door.

I signaled the waiter, who did not come running for me.

6

❦❦❦❦❦❦❦

I BROKE THE TAX SEAL on the fifth of
Gilbey's and spilled some over ice, where it went to work
like Prestone. Among an assortment of leftovers in my re-
frigerator, which were beginning to look like petri dishes, I
found a geriatric liter of tonic and watered the gin. Then I
took the glass, clinking in my hand, out to the apartment's
little screened porch overlooking woods and a slice of the
Concord River.

In theory it was romantic, but the river is a far cry from
the one Thoreau rowed down with his brother John a
hundred and fifty years ago, strangled now with soda cans,
bald tires, shopping carts, and weekenders in rubber rafts.
I sat there listening to the Red Sox on someone's radio,
and crickets, and every few seconds, the bitter crackle of
an insect hitting the blue zapper in a nearby back yard. It
seemed a cruel fate, rushing in, in the happy heat of yearn-
ing, then having your lights put out.

I built another drink, still easy on the G, generous with
the T.

If I boned up on my Freud, maybe I could make a case
for Joel Castle hitting on Lauren—some kind of childhood
transference issue, or revenge for old and unremembered
hurts done him—but I didn't buy it, and with the fourth

drink I futzed around the kitchen for awhile before I saw the drawer in the counter and knew I'd been coming to it all evening.

It's the drawer that collects everything, as basic to a home as a sink. I tugged it open and gazed in at twine, pencils with gnawed points, warranty cards that never got mailed, a tattered Lew Archer novel, packets of garden seeds, a jackknife, matchbooks (to which I added one from the 99, less a match), clipped recipes for quick 'n' easy meals I hadn't gotten around to making, expired coupons, assorted loose screws and nails, buttons, nail-clippers, chalk line, more pencils. In the back, under a postcard saying 'Sun your buns in Jamaica,' I found the flat, snap-lid box.

The shield hadn't been retired to the Crime Busters Hall of Fame, nor had anyone come to fetch it. I plucked it from the blue velour and tested it in my palm. I read the city motto printed above the city seal in good old English: *Art Is the Handmaid of Human Good.* I set the shield back. I looked at the three commendations, the ribbons a little more faded since the last time. The papers that went with them were around somewhere too. I closed the box and re-interred it in the drawer. I refilled my glass and went out on the porch. I thought about Lauren. I listened to the night chorus. Evening and a drink and time to sit and ponder. They were the small things you still had when you got derailed.

For no reason I was aware of, I thought about Bhuntan Tran. I thought how he must have sat like this in his own little microchip of heaven and listened to the sounds, sounds he had traded in the screams and the gunfire of the killing fields for. But the trade-in had been revoked; someone had seen to that. His American dream had turned to

46

nightmare. All at once, with the sudden brief clarity that booze brings, I realized that it was important to me to find out why Tran had died.

I thought about this a little more, but the clarity soon blurred.

After a while I went back inside and built another drink with a whole new blueprint.

7

❦❦❦❦❦❦❦

THE TELEPHONE WOKE me at five past eight, gritty-eyed and with teeth that felt like rocks in the old mill stream.

"Ho ho ho, Merry Christmas. You awake?"

"Whaa?"

"I got some information you wanted," Bob Whitaker, my photographer friend, said.

"Uhnh."

"You sound like you could use some strong coffee."

"Can."

"The Owl in twenty minutes?"

"Double it."

After I showered and got the moss scrubbed off, I put on a pale gray shirt, a black knit tie and my seersucker. Subdued seemed to be the hue of the day. Avoiding the debris in the kitchen where the Gilbey's bottle sat on the table, as dry as the drinks I'd faded out with last night, I forged outside into light rain. I got the bomber going and put it up on the Connector, which was a ruby necklace of brake lights. The world seemed to be moving like I was this morning, a foot at a time.

The small parking lot in front of the Owl Diner was crowded. Inside I found Bob Whitaker leaning at the cash register chatting with an orange-haired stringbean I hadn't seen before.

"Heeey," he greeted. "Lazarus comes forth."

A booth opened up in a corner, and we took it. The place was busy with building tradesmen rained out for the morning. They sat and drank coffee and swapped tales of construction woe. Outside the damp wind flagged the green awnings, and in here the windows fogged and it was pleasant. Whitaker is a short, brown man with an afro and an ability to win friends anywhere. Favoring loose army surplus clothing in drab tones, he blends in. You spot him snooping around town with the *Sun's* Nikons, but his true love is the old solid-body Leica he uses to shoot his own stuff.

Doris, one of the regular waitresses, brought coffee. I ordered a bran muffin while Whitaker asked for the works. From the pocket of her apron, Doris slipped out a booklet called *Zodiac Love Guide.*

"Hey, Rasmussen," she said, "what's your sign?"

I didn't have to think. " 'Quiet, Hospital Zone' is one I'm into today."

"*Tch.* Bob, what about you? When were you born?"

"February thirty-first," Whitaker told her.

She started to thumb pages, then caught on. Guys in the adjoining booth got into it. "Hey, Doris, my sign is 'free breakfast served all day.' "

"And free something else."

Doris cocked a fist on her hip and swept us all with a stare. Couldn't men ever take anything seriously?

When the food came, Whitaker went at his with appetite. I chewed the muffin deliberately, visualizing the bran trapping poisons in my system. The little carrot-top cashier came over with her name printed on a meal check and handed it to Bob with a smile. I gave him a look. "I took her picture," he said. "I'm going to send her one."

She headed back to the register. "Did you catch the freckles?" he asked. "And that smile? Like an angel by Botticelli. What bone structure."

"She'll make a beautiful skeleton."

"You're high-fivin' this morning."

"I saw Lauren last night."

He looked at me and said nothing more, knowing I'd give it if I needed to. Bob and his wife, Anne, had been our first neighbors when they moved from the South Shore. They knew the two of us and had kept the doors open both ways after our split.

"More to the point," I said, "I've got to see Fred Meecham, Esquire, today. There's no win in fighting."

Whitaker nodded. He was a talker, but he listened more than most people, and he caught details. He bitched and moaned and talked about getting out of Lowell and the newspaper racket and maybe hitting the road with Anne and their two kids. And he had the talent to take him as far as he wanted it to, I just wasn't sure he wanted. He'd have spit in my eye if I told him he had the makings of a lifer, but I had seen it happen with this place. Some people fell in love with sunlight on old brick, yesterday's news blowing in the street, girderwork bridges spanning the big river. And greasy spoon diners in tasty abundance. Doris brought more coffee, and the conversation turned to what he had exhumed from the *Sun*'s files.

In the past twelve months, besides Bhuntan Tran's, there had been six murders of Cambodians that had made the wire services and so had come up in the files he'd checked. Two each in San Francisco and Houston, one in Stockton, one in Seattle. Five men and a woman. "Plus I got one Laotian and two Vietnamese."

"Give me the Cambodians first."

"The most recent were Houston, in late May. Separate crimes, both victims males, and like all the others, they'd been shot. None of the crimes was solved as of the time they got reported. I did get a name of a cop who was handling the two in Texas."

He was a Lieutenant Nathan Rosenheck. I took the name down, as well as the names and ages of the victims in all nine cases, plus the dates of the killings and a few other details that Whitaker had got.

"You think it's a serial killer?" he asked.

"Wouldn't be my first guess." There was a definite gang structure. We had it in Lowell, punks preying on other Southeast Asians who worked for a living. The cops kept a pretty firm hand on them, but it was still an alien culture, not always easy to read.

As Botticelli's angel took my money, Doris sneaked up and peeked over my shoulder at the driver's license in my wallet.

"October seventeenth," she declared triumphantly. "Libra." She did a quick shuffle of pages. " 'Romance is indicated. Your love prospects are strong.' "

Bob caught my eye and piped in, "I'm Pisces, Doris."

She found the page. " 'You're going on a journey and meeting mysterious women.' "

"Nothing fishy about that. The *Sun* is sending me over to Fort Devens this afternoon to shoot the Officer Wives' Club strawberry festival."

"Y'see?" Doris crowed, vindicated.

I slotted the wheels in front of the Christian Science Reading Room and went into my building carrying black coffee in a paper cup. The elevator button responded with a Bronx cheer. I spotted the index card by my shoe. With vast labor I retrieved it and saw the hand-printed OUT OF ORDER of Fred Meecham, Esq. Probably something he had picked up in a courtroom. The dab of tape had dirt and hairs stuck to it, so I propped the card over the push button and hoped Fred had called the landlord. All that done, I gazed around the sad lobby, debating. But it's a tough call when phoning in sick would only get you your own tape machine. I put my legs to work on the stairs, concentrating on the worn brown patch in the middle of each green-carpeted tread, like the spot where Williams used to stand in left field at Fenway. I wondered if the Splendid Splinter had ever played feeling this rotten.

The waiting room wasn't exactly SRO. In fact it was empty, which for a change lifted me. I unlocked the office and went in and had dropped into my chair before I spotted the light blinking on my machine.

Ada Stewart had called to say she was to appear in juvenile court, which would tie up most of the day, but she would be back at DSS after five-thirty for at least an hour and would try me then. I wondered if I still heard the confidence in me she had walked away with yesterday. I couldn't decide.

I dug out the name Whitaker had given me and called long distance information and got the central number for the Houston Police. A woman with a voice like a windmill creaking in a Panhandle wind told me I'd gotten through and that my call was being recorded. She said Lieutenant Rosenheck was out of the office. I left my name and number, invoking Sergeant St. Onge; not lying, but maybe letting the woman believe I was with the Lowell PD. Sometimes you can Rockford it, but if the bluff backfires you get zip. Honest omission was more practical.

It was nine-thirty. I finished the coffee, then steeled myself for the three-story descent.

* * *

With the breeze from clocking sixty on I-93, my head finally started to clear, though no such luck for the sky, which went right on glowering, just enough rain spitting out of it to make the wipers squeak after a few strokes and keep me switching them off and on. I hung in behind a tractor-trailer with a yellow sign on the back that asked: HOW'S MY DRIVING? and gave an 800 number. I was in Wilmington in fifteen minutes.

TecStrand, Inc., was one of the low, glass-and-brick operations nestled off the highway behind screens of evergreen. Invisible to speeding traffic two hundred feet away, it was probably pinpointed on defunct target maps in the old war room of the Kremlin. I wheeled past the idle BMWs and Audis and occasional Benzo in the reserved lot and put the Bobcat next to a Jag. Keep the big felines together. I only hoped the Jag owner wasn't a door-banger.

In the smoked-glass entry I touched my tie, brushed rain off my face, then strolled into the lobby. A Cher look-alike without the edge smiled from a reception desk. "May I help you, sir?"

I gave her my name and said I had a ten o'clock appointment with Mr. Turcotte. She said if I would like to have a seat she would tell him I was there. "Help yourself to coffee."

I passed and wandered over to a glossy marble wall where there was a PR display on TecStrand. Teamwork was the company's biggest asset, I learned. I also learned that headquarters was in Little Rock. The Wilmington facility was chemical manufacturing—synthetic fibers for textiles and medical applications.

At a jingling sound I turned and saw a fiftyish man in a rumpled lab frock moving my way. The frock hung open over a pale yellow shirt and tired gray corduroys with a clip-on beeper and a big ring of keys. If keys were status, he was a CEO.

"Mr. Rasputin?" he said.

Nice talk when he was the one looking like a mad monk. I set him straight and we shook hands. He had the look I'd have if I didn't curb my ways—sallow, suspicious eyes and broken capillaries netting his cheeks. He wasn't much cheerier than I was this morning.

"What was it you wanted?" he asked.

I went through my intro. As soon as I mentioned Tran, his face shut down like the window shades of an old maid's bedroom. "I don't get it," he said. "The police are investigating. Why you?"

"An individual hired me."

He looked doubtful. "You're licensed to investigate a murder?"

"Not really. It's a cooperative arrangement. Look, if you've got problems with it, call Detective St. Onge at the Lowell Police."

He didn't look any less distrustful, but he wasn't going to bother to make the call. "So what can I say about Bhuntan Tran," he paraphrased me. "That he was a hard worker and an adequate technician."

"That sounds like faint praise," I said. "I understand Tran's specialty was environmental engineering."

Turcotte checked it for hooks, shrugged. "He was doing simple lab work here. He could've had a degree in flower arranging."

"Were you close?"

"You don't get close to people in this work. You do your job and keep an eye open for where the knife's going to come from."

I glanced around. "The knife?"

54

"Oh, it'll come. I guarantee it."

"I guess you didn't write the company promo about teamwork," I said.

"Look, you want the truth? This business is a jungle, same as any other. As for Tran, I hated the slope-headed little son of a bitch."

His testimonial was interrupted by a shrill beeping. He flapped open his smock and deactivated the page-call clipped to his belt. "Maria," he called to the woman with Cher hair. "Check three-one-seven for me."

She did, then called over her glass divider. "They want you in the gas lab."

"Do this, do that. They're running me goddamn ragged. I've got to go."

"Mind if I tag along? To see where Tran worked?"

He gave me an unhappy glance. "Okay. But you stay where I say. There's security work going on."

At the end of a long, rubber-tiled corridor that smelled strongly of sulphur, a woman came out of a door and conferred briefly with Turcotte. He said to her, "Take this guy into C lab and show him Tran's work station," then he disappeared through the door she had come out of.

The woman led me into one of the open labs and pointed at a lot of machines and glass piping, which meant nothing to me and even less after her brief explanation. She was an earnest, pretty woman of middle years and, according to the lapel button on her smock, committed to saving the ozone layer. "You knew Bhuntan?" she asked.

"I never met him." I told her why I was there. Maybe I should get small yellow cards made up: HOW'S MY DETECT-ING? and a toll-free number.

She shook her head. "I don't believe that drug business either. He was a sweet man, from everything I've heard."

"Mr. Turcotte doesn't seem to think so."

55

She appeared to consider whether to say more, then decided. "Norm was a good chemist for a lot of years. Believe it or not, his was once a name in synthetic fibers and plastics. He was very big."

So was the Hula Hoop, I thought. "What happened?"

"A colleague at another company took some formulas Norm had developed and stole all the credit. Norm never got over it. He became very distrustful, never worked well on a team again. But that was a long time ago. He's still a top-notch technician. Unfortunately, the man's worn out. At this stage in his life, he simply doesn't want the competition from anyone."

"Was Tran competition?"

"He was bright and capable. But this wasn't his field. He was just a hard worker."

"Any chance of my looking at his employment file?"

"You could check with personnel. Ask at the front desk. Under the circumstances, they might allow it."

I thanked her and went out. Turcotte appeared at the door of the other lab looking no less harried than before. "Lois, I'm going to need you." He glanced at me. "I'm in this up to my elbows. I told you everything I know anyway."

I watched him go back in, scared to death of his own demons. I found my way out all by myself.

8

⟨⟨⟨⟨⟨⟨⟨⟨⟨

THE ACRE USED to be the Greek section, back when the Greeks followed the French Canadians who had followed the paddy camp Irish as the immigrant wave washing into the city to work. The Olympia restaurant, with its Zorba Room, was still there, and a few small stores where you could buy Calamata olives and *mizithra* and over a glass of ouzo grouse with the proprietor about death and taxes. Like their predecessors, the Greeks who had prospered had moved to better neighborhoods, leaving the hard streets behind. Puerto Ricans, Cambodians, and Laotians lived there among the canals now, in ragged wooden tenements and their bunker-like counterparts, which locals had dubbed Cement City. I parked in front of a market with faded posters in the window in the curlicue typography of a language I didn't recognize, touting a month-old event. As I scanned building numbers, I observed a trio of men conducting a business transaction in a doorway of one of the project houses. They weren't trading stock tips. Down here *hostile takeover* had whole new shades of meaning.

On his job application in the personnel office at Tec-Strand, under "whom to notify in case of an emergency," Bhuntan Tran had listed Samol and Mai Lim. There was no hint as to who these people were, but he had given a telephone number. I had called ahead and struggled with making myself understood. Finally I suggested that it might be easier if I came by in person. I think the woman on the line understood me.

Number 402 was a three-story wooden building painted battleship gray. There were no screens on the windows, and bright curtains waved in many of them like semaphore flags. *Help* might have been the message they spelled out. In front stood a cluster of Southeast Asian youths. We checked each other without making eye contact; there was no threat in it, only mutual awareness. I went into the hallway, where I scanned a lot of foreign names on the scabbing mailboxes and pressed a bell button for apartment D. I had no idea if it rang anywhere until I spotted four small heads peering over a top floor railing at me, like dark mops set to dry. Then two only slightly taller people appeared, a young woman with glossy black hair and an older, gray version of her.

"Mrs. Lim?"

The young woman gave a smile that looked pained. "Come up stair if you please."

They made a little aisle for me, and I went into a kitchen with sparkling linoleum and a big table covered with an orange vinyl table cloth. Mai Lim ushered me through tied-back curtains into an adjoining room. The kids scampered along like I was the Pied Piper. In addition to the four, who probably had sixteen years among them, there was a slightly older girl, maybe ten, plus Mrs. Lim, and the old woman and an equally wrinkled man, who she said were her mother and father. The old man pushed himself up on a cane to join the others in watching me respectfully as I stood in their apartment. His right pant leg was knotted ten inches from his hip and hung empty.

"Please, sir, sit," I said, though I was pretty sure it was my gesture and not the words he responded to. Only Mai Lim and the children seemed to know English. The little kids went off to play. The ten-year-old hunkered down on her haunches under a playbill for a film called *12 Sisters* and a Batman poster.

The grandmother brought in a kitchen chair for me, and rather than argue chivalry, I sat. The ten-year-old went on staring at me the way a child will watch a magician, looking for the trick. I said to Mai Lim, "I understand you and your husband were friends of Bhuntan Tran."

"We friend of Bhuntan. Very good man."

"How long did you know him?"

"My husband know Bhuntan since they take class here to become American citizen. Then I come to join too." She smiled broadly. "I'm citizen soon."

Her pride in this moved me. "Congratulations."

"Thank you very much."

"So Bhuntan was not a relative. A brother or sister or cousin," I added to avoid confusion. "He was a friend."

"Yes. We love him very much. He come in our home many time. His family was kill in Cambodia before he go to Thailand and then coming here." She was still smiling and I realized it must be a form of politeness. "Bhuntan good friend," she said again, and again I felt an admiration bordering on affection for a man I would never meet. He had survived horrors only to succumb here in the promised land.

I felt lousy bringing up the next topic.

"What about drugs. Did Bhuntan use drugs?"

Mai Lim and the old woman exchanged words, and I saw what looked awfully like expressions of disapproval—of me or the drugs or Bhuntan, I wasn't sure. Mai Lim said, "No drug. In Cambodian home, family very important. When man and woman marry, priest he tell them— no longer say, 'I.' Always 'we.' When man and woman join, they speak, 'we.' " She pressed her small brown hands together. "No drug. We think drug very bad thing. Bhuntan—no drug." The old woman showed her gold teeth and seconded this in vigorous Khmer.

I dropped the topic. "Bhutan had a relative in California," I said. "A cousin."

She frowned. "I'm not think so. All family kill in Cambodia."

I dug out my notebook and showed her the name I had copied at the mortgage office. Suoheang Khoy. "*Swang Coy*" is how she pronounced it. She shook her head. "I do not know him."

"Did Bhuntan have enemies?"

She thought about that one. "Enemy, no. Not here. In Cambodia, very many enemy for all of us. Khmer Rouge. Terrible. Here we live in peace."

The old man spoke for the first time and the adults conducted a three-way conversation, the ten-year-old cupped her mouth and snickered. A couple words sounded familiar, but I told myself, no way.

Mai Lim interpreted. "Father say you detective like Magnum, P.I."

I grinned at the old-timer. "Give or take the moustache and Ferrari."

He grinned back with perfect incomprehension.

"Ferrari," I heard the little girl say softly, and I realized the reason for her attentiveness. This was a vocabulary lesson.

"That red car Magnum drives is a Ferrari," I told her. She gave me a shy smile. Mr. Rogers had nothing on me.

I asked a few more questions and left open the possibility of speaking with Mai Lim's husband Samol sometime. On the landing outside the door, with the kids lining up again, Mai Lim gave me a pained look of questioning. "It not fair," she said. "We here, Bhuntan gone. Why anyone kill Bhuntan?"

I wished I had an answer for her. "I don't know," I said.

"You find out?"

What did you say to that except that you would do your best?

I brought a sandwich back to the office. Lieutenant Rosenheck of the Houston PD had returned my call. I bounced another one his way and missed. We were on the court at least, only playing different matches. I hauled over the typing table, snapped the dustcover off the Royal, rolled paper into it, and began to log the day's events.

I use the notes to undergird a better-than-fair memory, and for the detailed reports I provide clients upon completion of an investigation. Sometimes, as now, the notes reminded me of something so obvious I forgot it now and again. Reality is relative. It's the elephant and the blind men. What you tried to do was come at a problem from as many ways as made sense, and even a few that didn't. Through the gradual buildup of detail, the superimposing of layers, you got an approximation of reality. That was just beginning to happen for me with Bhuntan Tran.

I had the testimony of Ada Chan Stewart, of Claire Azar and hubby Joe, of Perry at the laundry, of Cassie Samms, Norm Turcotte and his assistant, Lois, and Mai Lim. Each view was doubtless distorted to some degree; and I'd handicap Joe Azar and Turcotte a few points for general sourness. The result was an emerging portrait of

61

Tran. Truth? Objective reality? No, but more than I'd had yesterday. Like a print in the developing tank, something was starting to take form. I put my notes into a file folder.

When I finished my sandwich and coffee, I dragged out into the light something that had been crouching in a corner of my mind all day. With it, my skull gave a last throb, and then the pain was gone. There would be other pain to come, but it would locate itself elsewhere. Given time and luck, that ache might fade too. I went down the hall to attorney Fred Meecham's office. I told him what I wanted. He asked just once if I was sure I shouldn't play hardball. I said I was sure, and he got a few points of detail and said he'd have paper ready for signature in a day or two. When I took out my wallet he scowled.

As I stepped back through my waiting room, the phone was ringing.

"Howdy, Rasmussen?" said a voice that was familiar.

"Speaking."

"Nate Rosenheck here."

It was familiar from my tape machine. "Thanks for getting back," I said.

"What can I do you for, partner?" He had a deep Texas drawl that made me feel like a caller on a radio advice show: *Y'see, Calvin, I've got this mail-order pickle business, and . . .*

I said, "I got your name from a news account of some killings you had in late May. I wanted to ask a few questions."

"You work with . . ." I heard paper rustle, "Sergeant St. Onge." He gave it a hard *g* and an *ee* sound at the end, but I let it go, since they weren't likely ever to meet.

"Formerly. I'm private now." I explained the current

arrangement, which he didn't seem to have any problem with. He wasn't one of these small-bore papercrats who get so hung up on jurisdictions they'd rather see the bad guys walk than cut someone else a piece of case.

"What are y'all looking for?" he asked.

"I'm not sure." I briefed him on the Tran killing. "No motive or suspects yet."

He grunted. "We haven't found anything for our two either. You have any gangs operating up your way?"

"There's an occasional something running between here and Providence. Car theft is big, home invasions. You think a gang's involved?"

"Nah. They're mostly punks, too stupid to know that being tough's got nothing to do with violence. The victims here were older than that." Of the two in Houston, he said, one had been shot with a handgun at close range, the other with a rifle. He knew about the killings in California and Seattle.

Something got me thinking, and I reached over to my bookcase while he talked.

"Funny you called, Rasmussen. Few days back I telexed the PDs in those other cases to request police and ballistics reports. I ought to be hearing soon."

"So you wonder if there might be a bigger picture?"

"The thought occurs."

I had the Rand McNally atlas open on my desk, my finger touring California. "Drugs involved in any of the others?"

"Inconsistent. Some coke in a few, and now yours. Be honest with you, I don't see a strong pattern. Down here we spend a half-zillion dollars to have a symphony orchestra and an art museum, and probably half again as much for the joys of guns and drugs. What can I tell you?"

"We're a fun-loving society."

"Yup."

"So you think I'm spitting in the wind?"

"Hey, if you can shut a few files by coming up with a pattern that makes sense, go for it. If it don't fit, let's try another tune."

I let the mixed metaphor go and played my long card. "Does the name Souheang Khoy jingle any bells?" I gave the name the sound Mai Lim had and spelled it.

"Y'all saying it should?"

"He's an acquaintance or a relative of the man who got gunned here," I said. "His name came up in a mortgage application file because he gave Tran five thousand dollars a few years ago to buy a house. He's from San Jose, which isn't too too far from San Francisco or Stockton. Big deal, huh?"

"I got the name down. Won't hurt to check. Anything else?"

"I wish there were."

Either he'd just thought of it, or he'd taken his time getting there. "Did y'all notice anything more about the gunshots?"

"Like?"

"Don't know. Look, would you ask St. Onge to get me a copy of his report, including the death certificate?"

It had been the latter. He'd guessed I hadn't eyeballed the report. "I'll ask him."

"I'd be obliged. Maybe we'll be in touch."

I put the atlas back on the shelf with my collection of phone directories, road maps and take-out menus. I got an idea. But first I placed a call to the Immigration and Naturalization Service number in Boston. A recorded voice told me that practically anything I'd ever want to know about INS was contained in a series of taped messages, all I needed to do was signal by punching in three-digit codes whenever I wanted to hop off, and then I was gone, hooked into a tape loop that promised to go on and on. It was probably an improvement over the old days when government phones would ring forever; but even getting through was no guarantee of anything. Conversations with the government could turn into Abbott and Costello routines. I let the loop ride for a few minutes. Not finding anyplace I wanted to visit, I cradled the phone.

I brought the Royal back for round two. I'd go after them in cold print.

A quick klackety-klack, listing the names of the Cambodian victims, requesting information that might connect them, thank you very much, yours, Citizen Rasmussen. With luck I'd hear by Labor Day. I mailed the letter across the street, then shagged my car.

9

〰〰〰〰〰

ONE PLACE WHERE you could always
find parking space was in front of the city library. I used
the card catalog, then the non-fiction stacks, where I un-
shelved several books that appeared to be personal recol-
lections of life in Cambodia during its fall. One was called
To Destroy You Is No Loss, from a snappy little saying of the
Khmer Rouge which went, "To keep you is no benefit; to
destroy you is no loss." I settled at a long table with my
pad and pencil. For a while I scribbled notes, then I got
pulled in and just read. When I remembered where I was,
it was 5:40. I signed out the book, thanked the librarian
for her hospitality, and went outside to find my meter
overrun. A ticket smiled at me from under the wiper. I
could put it on the tab as an expense, I supposed, but
it was my own stupidity, so I'd eat it. Teach a man to
read . . .

I drove out Lawrence to the six hundred block, where
the Department of Social Services branch office sat, a
two-story beige clapboard building with an outside staircase, reminiscent of an Army barracks. It was five minutes
before metered parking lapsed for the day, but I plugged a
coin in anyway. Two bits against a sawbuck made sense.
As I walked to the building, a short, trim man of middle

years was locking the front door. He was wearing a green Izod shirt and chinos with a page-call clipped to his belt. He had freckled arms and neatly brushed sandy-gray hair.

"Hi, has Ada Stewart gone for the day?" I asked him.

He sized me up through photobrown glasses with gold frames. "Friend?"

"Friend*ly*. We're working on something together."

He grinned and unlocked the door again. "Ada's back yonder, doing paperwork."

"Still?"

"That's one thing about this job just won't quit—and ever'one wants their cc yesterday. I'm Walt Rittle, by the way. One of the old burnouts Ada's stuck with." He thrust a hand at me and I took it and introduced myself.

"Jeezum, it's a high-wire act, this job," he went on. "But I figure it's the peoplework, the contact with the client that means something at the end of the day. The paper gets done when it gets done." He had the amiable, indefinably Southern accent that people acquire when they have put in years bouncing around for the government. I had heard a lot of it in the Army. "Well, I'm off to one more client—family case we can get together only in the evening when the old man's home. You take care."

The ground floor of DSS was a large bullpen with lots of desks and lots of paper on the desks. No one was sitting at any of them. At the rear was a copy machine and a row of flimsy-looking cubicles. Ada Stewart was in the second one back, standing over a computer screen, a little V of perplexity crinkling her forehead. She was wearing a denim skirt with a halter top over a pink leotard. She didn't look up.

"Walter, I thought you left."

"He did."

She glanced up in surprise. "Oh, Mr. Rasmussen." She straightened. "Come in." She gestured me into the cramped little work space, where files were stacked alongside heaps of printout.

"You're going to give government employees a bad name. Aren't you supposed to be smoke at four thirty-one?"

"Walter ruins that around here. He's the most energetic social worker I've ever known."

"Look who's talking."

She flushed slightly and smiled. "I'm glad you came by. I'm dying to hear what you've found out. Please sit."

She moved some papers, and I straddled a chair as she took her own seat. I told her how she'd spent her money the past two days.

"You've covered a lot of ground," she said when I'd finished.

I lifted a shoulder. "What's it amount to? For all his low profile, Tran seems to have left his mark. He stirred up a lot of admiration, loyalty, hatred, jealousy, even love."

"He was a remarkable person."

"I'm a little sorry I didn't know him."

"So you do believe me about the drugs?"

"Fingerprints notwithstanding? I'm inclined to," I said. "Though where's the proof? I don't think you'll really find any."

"Short of his killer being found?"

I granted the possibility.

"I'd like to keep you working on it," she said.

"I wouldn't feel right taking your money."

Her eyes were penetrating, intelligent, and . . . shy? Oh, hell, inscrutable. Her face was less round and flat than Chinese, less sharp than Caucasian; her hair dark. She was a greatest-hits album.

"Do you know who my family are?" she asked.

"Yeah. Sergeant St. Onge gets credit for the brilliant discovery."

"But you understand money isn't really an issue."

"It is with me. You asked me yesterday what kind of work I specialize in. There are jobs I like doing, and a few I don't, but my specialty is anything that comes in the door. It would be a sore temptation to string you along with promises that I'll fulfill all your expectations. The truth is I probably can't."

"Who says I'd need them all fulfilled?" she asked, meeting my gaze.

I took a pass on that one.

"I mean, look what you've accomplished already," she said.

"About all I can. There might be a couple more phone calls, a little more shoe leather, another paragraph in my report. But your best card is still the one you've had all along."

She looked away. "The police."

"You've already paid for them."

She said nothing for a moment. In the outer office a telephone rang half a dozen times, then quit. Abruptly, Ada turned to her computer. Unlike the Royal in my office, the keys *queek*ed as she pecked them. From the angle I was sitting at I saw clusters of words and numbers begin swarming the screen.

" 'Rosita Lopes,' " Ada read off the monitor, "from the Azores. Nguyen Thoc, Vietnam. Teeda and Boreth Leng, Cambodia by way of a Thai refugee camp. Haiti. Cambodia again. Puerto Rico." She looked at me. "They come here with dreams, Mr. Rasmussen. But they get a big dose of reality too—the kind you won't see featured in the four-color brochures from the Chamber of Commerce. No job, poor English skills, substandard housing, prejudice."

"Maybe they should think twice about coming," I said.

"Some of them, yes. We don't need people who won't follow the rules, or who are looking only to stay on these rolls. But that's not the majority. People can usually make it if they get their feet under them. But to do that they need more than just Walter Rittle or me. They need hope, because it's easy to give up and go down. Then we've *all* got a problem. A Bhuntan Tran stands for hope. Dammit, I want to see him keep standing."

The energy and heat of her words withered my smart retort. With the dough her family was worth, she could be anywhere, doing anything, instead of sitting here in this two-by-four office making me feel guilty because my contribution amounted to little more than the taxes I shipped off each quarter. I stood up, jingling change with my pocketed hands. "There'd be no guarantees."

"Are there ever?" Her tone softened. "Stay on it, that's all I'm asking. Do those last few things you mentioned, whatever they are. What will it take you, another day? Two?"

"I might turn up something."

She stood too, watching me with wry, inquiring eyes. "You're not completely booked, are you?"

So what do you say? I said, "You drive a tough bargain, lady," and I grinned.

She took out her checkbook, but I held up a hand. "You've retained me already. The bill comes with my final report. I'll be in touch." I started for the door.

"Mr. Rasmussen?"

Shyness had reclaimed her, leaving only the afterglow of intensity on her cheeks, and for an instant I thought she would tell me never mind. She said, "Are you going back to work already?"

"I thought I'd go catch and kill dinner first," I said.

Her small, sturdy fingers worried a paperclip. "Do you ever eat with clients . . . or is there a rule?"

I shrugged. "It's neater than eating with my hands."

10

⊘⊘⊘⊘⊘⊘⊘⊘

THE APPLETON INN has improved
since it opened, having learned that fancy rooms are not
enough to get the business trade if you are not the only
show in town. The modern commercial traveler is too
savvy about food to settle strictly for proximity. Tonight
the dining room wasn't busy. A pair of tables had been
drawn together to accommodate a party of visiting fire-
people with name tags on their lapels. Ada Chan Stewart
and I got a table in a corner. The brass and the fox and
hounds prints gave a nice faraway feel to the place. The
waiter lit the candle in the tall glass chimney and said that
the swordfish had just come in. I ordered that. Ada Stewart chose lobster.

"Are you married, Mr. Rasmussen?" she asked me
when the waiter had poured wine.

"Is this social work?"

"Personal curiosity. Tell me to mind my own business if
I'm overstepping."

"The answer is yes. Technically." I told her how things
were, up to and including Fred Meecham, Esq.'s, newest
assignment.

With only the subtlest shifting of planes her face showed
sympathy. "It's a tough world," she said. "It's easy to get
derailed in it."

"That *is* social work."

"I'll shut up."

"I was just thinking about something that Mai Lim said today—about a Cambodian couple not using 'I' in their home."

"Yes. After the wedding it's always supposed to be plural."

"Interesting custom. I don't recall a lot of 'we' over the last couple years of my marriage." I shrugged and let it go. "What about you?"

"Wed to work, I guess."

"Sounds one-sided."

"I don't know. It has its satisfactions."

"You have a private life?"

"From time to time. Low-maintenance relationships mostly. Dinner, a movie. Work occupies me pretty much. There's never any end of people in need."

"Don't you ever feel like the little Dutch kid?"

"Not often. And I don't imagine you do either."

"Not more than seven dikes a week."

She smiled, and I realized it wasn't an expression I'd seen a lot of on her face. I liked how it looked.

"But we don't give in to it," she went on, the smile fading.

"First person plural?"

"You, me, Walt Rittle—lots of others. You find us in every occupation. What we do is important. Each of us is just one person, but if we can do something for one other person today, it's enough. Tomorrow will have challenges of its own."

"You really feel like that?"

"I try to wake up each morning eager for what the day will bring."

"You weren't me waking up this morning."

"Okay, sure, every so often I think of chucking it all. I had this idea of going back to school . . . to study Egyptology, believe it or not."

"But why be practical?"

"Truthfully, Raz—" She stopped. "That came kind of naturally. Do people call you that?"

"A few have lived."

She gave away another short smile. "Seriously, it's a hurting world. Every one of us can do something to make it better. Yes, there are days when I grow weary. I'll be thirty-two in a few months. Sometimes I feel like I've been at this forever. But what are my alternatives? Lounge around the ancestral manor and send out for Chateaubriand?"

"These ancestors—they interviewing for a replacement?"

She tilted her head. "You're a tough man to have a serious conversation with."

"I had a serious conversation over dinner last night. Nothing kills appetite quicker."

She was looking at me in a way that happens between people once in a while, when the superficialities have proven needless. "You're funny, Alex." She paused. "I like the sound of that better."

I realized I did too; like I liked her smile. The food came. The appetite was hitting on all cylinders tonight. The swordfish was moist and sweet and almost as enjoyable as watching Ada Stewart in her bib cracking a big lobster. She wasn't of the new generation of women whose idea of eating hearty was a rice cake and a club soda. When we finished, we ordered coffee, and the waiter offered complimentary cordials. My friend Nan Crawford came over and slid into the booth beside me. She is one of those people who are completely without guile. She steps in, pushing her hip and large breasts against you, moving right into your space—though it isn't a come-on or a threat; Nan is just a warm life force.

"Rasmussen," she said, "you're a wonder."

"They're hoping to get De Niro to play me in the film version," I said. I introduced her to Ada.

"I ought to put you on retainer as a scout," Nan told me. "A million thanks for sending Cassie Samms."

"You like her?"

"To put it mildly. I'd have started her on the spot. I even offered her a bonus, but she said it was only right to give notice at the laundry. So she'll start in two weeks. And I'll still give her the bonus."

The three of us chatted about how hard it was to find good help, and the general decline of the West, until the desk clerk came and Nan had to go straighten out a reservation mix-up.

"You've got a friend," Ada said to me.

"When this place first opened, I helped Nan catch an employee who had sticky fingers. It was going to be hard to get around the union, and harder to get the kid to stop. One of the meat cutters is Lebanese, with an Old World sense of justice. I arranged for him to catch her in the till and threaten to take her hand off with a meat ax if he caught her again. The girl's a night clerk now and taking management courses at the university."

"Under the tough shell," Ada said, "you're a softie."

I winked. "So was that crustacean you just devoured."

We had another cup of coffee, then walked out into the indigo twilight. I drove her back to the DSS office and waited as she got into a little silver-gray Celica. She rolled the headlights on and waved. We drove off in different directions.

I cruised back through the city, out Bridge Street, and

crossed the river. Back on the other shore was what once had been a mile-long span of mills before arson and urban renewal had cut it by half; but the huge brick structures were still impressive. The last tinge of day lacquered the long rows of windows, and lights winked in the easy-flowing water. Peaceful. I put Sinatra in the tape deck and took the long way home.

11

~~~~~~~~~~

AT SEVEN A.M. the heat was a mocking promise. I had sweated through my T-shirt before I'd run a mile of the paved trail along the river. I could hear grasshoppers complaining from the weeds where the dew had already dried. As I approached the turnaround point at two miles, where another nest of condominiums had been slapped up, I noticed a wiry man in a nylon sweatsuit standing next to a small blue pickup truck parked beyond the barrier. He had his arms and knees slightly bent, and was posed like a lawn statue. As I neared, he relaxed and looked my way. Like-minded fools, trying to sweat on a hot morning, we waved to each other. When I made my turn, he said, "Hey, Mr. Rasmussen?"

I looked again and recognized the man I'd met yesterday afternoon at the DSS office, Ada's coworker.

"Walt Rittle," he said to refresh my memory.

I stopped and went over. Our hands made a wet grip.

"Hot enough for you?" he said. It was the kind of heat that brought the clichés, but who had the energy to be original? "You run down here a lot?"

"Just enough to keep the corpuscles from gridlocking," I said.

"I know what you mean. I do a little t'ai chi."

That's what it was, I realized now.

"God knows you need *something* when you're a chair-borne ranger most of the day," he said.

"Were you in the paratroops?"

He lifted his eyebrows. "Jeezum, you *are* a detective."

"So are you."

"Huh? Oh, Ada told me. Hope she wasn't giving anything away."

"She's paying the bills."

He laughed. "Yeah, I did a hitch with the Eighty-second Airborne. Then the lightbulb went on and I realized no way was I going to be able to keep up with all those lean tough kids. What about you?"

"Strictly a grunt, the draftee tour." I braced on the tailgate of his truck and leaned into a stretch. There was a tow-bar welded to the bumper with a faded tennis ball covering the ball hitch where I put one foot and bent the other knee.

"I used to think the Army was everything a man could want," Walt Rittle went on. "Three squares a day, a roof over your head, and you got fucked every day—pardon my French." His amiable grin faded. "Actually the service cost me my marriage. And then half my pay in alimony. I got out."

"Social work's easier?"

"I'm older and wiser." He winked. "So, how's that Bhuntan Tran business coming?"

"I'm older anyway." Generally I'd have left it at that, but it was possible Ada was too close to the case for any objectivity. Information is where you find it. "Walt, did you ever work with Tran too?"

"I knew about him, of course. He was well thought of in the Asian community. I never actually met him."

"Any opinion on the idea that he was a coke hound?"

"That's a tough call. Aside from what I read? I'd say no. But this here's America, where anything can happen."

We chatted another few minutes without settling the debate over heat versus humidity, then went back to just sweating.

By nine o'clock a haze hung thick over the city like a foretaste of what it was going to be like when we'd burned our final bridges. I could smell fluorocarbons as I got out of the car. Lady Earth was a big, loyal, good-hearted woman whom we'd been slapping around for a long time, but you could see her starting to sullen. It was there in the snap of her storms, the grumble of an earthquake, the steady burn of heat that scorched crops and killed cattle. She was turning, and if we didn't make up somehow, soon, she'd be gone for good. Under my suit coat my shirt was as sticky as a congressman's palm, and ozone stung my eyes as I climbed the steps of the JFK Civic Center.

Ed St. Onge stood before the window air conditioner, his arms spread like wings, gazing out.

"You won't get far," I said.

He turned. "You oughta call before coming."

"I was in the area."

He closed the door himself and moved back to his desk, parked a haunch and fingered his moustache. "So?"

I gave him a photocopy of my typed notes and filled him in on some of what I'd been doing the past two days. I asked if the cops had learned anything about the person Claire Azar saw coming out of the woods behind Tran's house.

"Neighbor on the next block says he spotted a small white car driving slowly down Prather Street that night.

79

He didn't catch the make or how many people were in it. Late model, sporty, he said, white wheel covers. No one else saw or heard diddly. That five grand you say someone gave Tran—could be the dough was for toot."

"I thought about that, but it doesn't fit the picture I'm getting."

"Maybe you're getting the wrong picture."

"With my powers of ratiocination? Reminds me, you forgot to tell me whether the M.E. found any drugs in Tran's system."

"And you're going to forget the answer."

"My memory isn't what it used to be."

"Clean," he said.

I looked at him. "Doesn't that shake loose your theory?"

"I give a shit if Tran was using. I think he was dealing."

I frowned. It wasn't anything I'd come across yet, but the discrepancies bothered me. If Tran was clean, as most of what I'd found so far seemed to say, where had the coke come from? Planted? And the money? "If not," I said, "and if the pro theory holds, the burn had to be for something else."

"What else?"

"A wrong done somebody? These people have a strong sense of personal honor. Feuds can go on a long time."

St. Onge scowled. "How about mistaken identity? They all look alike to me." He fanned out a match and huffed smoke.

"What's the matter, Ed?"

He spread a hand. "The Tran case is one of five I'm working. Count 'em. This damned heat . . ."

He glanced past my shoulder toward the closed door where a disembodied voice had drifted by.

"And the Ogre?" I said.

He met my eyes. "Yeah, maybe."

One of us—I couldn't remember who anymore—had come up with the handle. Droney had been a decent cop once, a long time ago, and had made his bones; but he'd soured. He had more moods than a teenage girl, most of them bad, and you never knew which he was in. The result was you trod carefully, alert for tripwires. "What's his problem?" I asked. "His yes-men telling him no?"

"He's a junkyard dog the last couple days. All over my back. Some of his pals next door are getting mentioned in a federal probe."

"Horrors. Dishonesty at city hall?"

"Go ahead, be smart. You don't work here."

"Redundant is what I'm being. And you're being something else. Abstruse? Is that a good word for the day?"

His cigarette smoldered, smoke ribboning thinly up to where currents from the air conditioner stirred it into the general station house funk.

"So where does the Tran case stand?" I asked.

He jabbed the butt out in his ashtray, freeing his hands to talk. He thumbed his chest. "My turn to wax literary. It's nearing the end of the term and report cards are due. You see half a dozen apples in a bowl, a bright shiny mac on top, down to a shriveled little crabapple on the bottom. Which one do you put on the teacher's desk?"

"Justice is blind," I said.

"I'm talking realities. You worked here once."

"Tran was just a refugee, not a pillar of the city, not even a good ordinary American with a name like Comtois, or O'Bannon . . . Sarantopoulos or Grabowski."

"You know that's not my view."

I did know. It wasn't even the view of the department,

81

which on balance was a fair organization. But there are behaviors that get institutionalized and it's nobody's fault and everybody's. St. Onge was on the home team. That's where his first loyalty lay. I said, "The cooperation we talked about the other day still good?"

"The investigation isn't closed, the effort's just in other places at the moment. I'll still try to help you out."

"It's 'try' now," I said.

"What do you need?"

"How about showing me—"

He cut me off with a hand. There was a rap and the door opened. Gus Deemys, looking cool and dapper in gray-green Italian silk, stepped in. Seeing me he stopped and glanced at St. Onge. "Interrupting something?"

"What's up, Gus?" St. Onge asked.

"Hancock on these?" Deemys waved some paper and came over and handed it to St. Onge. "No rush." As he started back he slid me a look with raised eyebrows. "I saw your wife the other day. Riding in a Rolls Royce. Joel Castle's car, I think."

I met his gaze with silence. He smiled it off and moved to the open door. When he got there he stopped. "Hey, I'd probably roll for a Rolls myself."

Possibly he had already turned away and didn't see me, or maybe I was moving that fast. I caught one unconstructed shoulder of suitcoat in my right hand and a narrow lapel in the left and wheeled him around. The silk tore. He gave a startled gasp, and his head clocked the glass brick wall. My knee paused a tender half-inch from putting him into the Greater Lowell Boys' Choir.

"Hey! Cut it!" St. Onge rushed over.

Not quick enough. Francis X. Droney filled the doorway of his office diagonally across the hall.

I gave Deemys's lapel another twist, then let go. He shoved my hands away and tugged his jacket into place like a cheerleader whose skirt had been ruffled by a fresh halfback, but he said nothing.

Droney's gaze had scanned the scene and come to rest on me. "The fuck you doing here?" he said.

Droney and I went way back; but I didn't want to get into it. I already felt bad for pulling St. Onge along. I shook my head. "Nothing."

A barrel-torsoed man with a ruff of hair the color of rusted steel, Droney had on brown slacks which broke on his shoes like muddy waves and one of the pilled half-sleeve Dacron shirts he wore year-round, with a tie as wide as a city councillor's smile. His laser stare didn't waver. "You're a coin-op cop now. What were you after?"

"Nothing," I said again.

I started toward the door, but he barred me. "Hold it, Coin-Op. I asked you a question. What're you here for?"

I sighed. "I was lodging a complaint," I said. "Someone stuck chewing gum on my office doorbell. It rings all day."

He gnawed on that for a nanosecond, then scowled at St. Onge and Deemys, who looked only beaten. I noticed that the bar that held his tie in place was a miniature pair of gold handcuffs. He looked back at me. "It don't matter shit what you were doing," he said, " 'cause none of this is going any farther. I guaran-fucking-tee it."

"Further."

He blinked. "What'd you say?"

Drop it, an inner voice said. " 'Farther' is for literal distance," I said. "You meant 'further.' "

Droney's heavy jaw worked, like that of an ox masticating bitter grass. Finally something twisted his mouth. A

83

smile. "I liked it better the last time you were in my office. Yeah, remember that?"

I wasn't likely to forget anytime soon. Droney and a few others had been there. There'd been pain in some of the faces, but not Droney's. He'd enjoyed himself. "I remember."

"Good, good. Because if you interfere with an investigation . . . you even show your sorry-ass face around here again, I'm going to ride over you like a dump truck. You got a few people to vouch for you before—" his glance cut St. Onge in "—so you managed to wangle a peeper's license. Big deal. I'll see you get squeezed faster than a pimple. I know people in Boston."

"Like you know people next door?"

He rocked a little, heel to toe, gripping the belt cinched over his hard-fat stomach and letting his heat cool through a tiny smile. He'd been a three-pack-a-day man for a lot of years and his teeth were stained like the porcelain of an old urinal. "I don't like you, mister," he said finally. "I never did."

"Damn! I hope I can get a refund on that Dale Carnegie course."

"Keep it up, hot shit."

But I was through. My control was unraveling. I wanted out of there.

Droney said, "The matter's shut. This isn't going any far—" I saw him hesitate "—anyplace but here. And don't give me that shit you don't work for me, you got a client paying you. Get in my way, I'll sling your sorry ass so high you'll need a step ladder to tie your shoes."

"I can't picture that."

"You wish." He skewered me with the stare. "You don't like it, you can kiss my rosy pink ass."

I caught St. Onge's look of warning and should have taken heed, but Droney and I had already crossed the line both of us had known we'd have to cross sooner or later.

"Point to a spot, Francis," I said. "From where I'm standing, you're all ass."

I walked away slower than I thought I could.

12

⦿⦿⦿⦿⦿⦿⦿⦿⦿

THE MORGUE FOR Middlesex County was in East Cambridge, a three-story cube of red brick with limestone lintels over peeling dark green sashes that looked like they hadn't been opened in forty years. People who ran such places were always fussy about flies. Fortunately, they weren't as careful about visitors.

A girl with shoe-polish–black hair and a matching leather tie on a white shirt sat at a desk with a television set the size of a ring box perched on it. Without ungluing her eyes from the screen, she said, "*All My Children.* Help yiz?"

"Why don't you videotape it at home," I said, "so you can go blind in peace?"

She popped her gum and looked up. "Kiddin' me? Then I'd have to wait'll I got off work to see what happens. Anyways, nighttime's party time."

It filled you with hope for America's future. "Is the big fellow still here?" I didn't remember his name, so I let my arms describe him.

"Al LaRosa. He's here."

"That settles a bet. A buddy of mine told me Al had gone on some weird diet and was riding Thoroughbreds at Suffolk Downs."

Nothing fazes them. Having grown up on soaps and

MTV, they've seen it all. The gum kept popping. "No, he's here. You want to see Al?"

"Please."

It was an echoey staircase of glazed firebrick and pipe railing sweating in the heat. Unless the place had changed, left at the bottom would take you into cold storage and the smell of strong disinfectant, and lamps that made shadows jump in the corners every time you turned. It hadn't. I saw the tin-sheathed double doors with their counterweights and umpteen coats of green paint. The dead don't need windows. I was happy to turn right.

A varnished wooden door with a wire-reinforced glass pane opened into a bright warren with a chest-high counter setting off a small work area. Beyond it receded the shelves of county death records. In the middle ground, behind his desk, sat Al LaRosa.

He looked the same as he had the last time I saw him, which had to be five years, give or take forty pounds. On him it didn't show. He was the size of a Dumpster, wearing a straw fedora and a pale yellow wash-and-wear shirt. It was refreshingly cool there, out of the July sun, but he was dripping on the *Herald* spread open to the racing form.

He'd been there for a decade that I knew of, ever since I was a uniform and had to come for the first time after an indigent woman had been pulled from one of the canals. Accidental drowning was the ruling that time. There had been other times, but now I got the feeling that LaRosa only dimly recognized my face. He probably wouldn't know I didn't carry a badge these days.

"Long time," he said in his rusty, Andy Devine voice.

I grinned hello and bellied up to the counter. "Never long enough as far as most visitors are concerned, I bet."

His chair groaned. "Here to ID someone?"

"Just an M.E.'s report on a homicide victim."

"Don't you get a copy at the station? You're Arlington, right? Or Somerville."

"Lowell. Rasmussen's the name."

"Yeah, that's it."

"But I'm private these days." I opened the manila folder on the linoleum countertop and futzed importantly with papers.

He adjusted his hat. " 'Course, autopsy reports are considered medical files now. State law says they're protected from public disclosure."

"This is official," I said, stretching it. "I'm working in connection with Frank Droney."

"That son of a whore?"

"Can I quote you?"

"You certainly can. I hope I see the day he ends up in here, bagged and tagged."

"Too bad we have to wait."

He gave me a look. Maybe there was a stir of memory of who I'd ended up being. The Boston papers had given the story a pretty good ride, though cop corruption was getting to be old news. After a moment, LaRosa lumbered from his chair and moved the five feet to the counter. "Homicide, you said?"

I pointed at Tran's name on the top of my sheet. I tried to keep it from getting dripped on. LaRosa said, "Lowell. The Chinese fellow."

"Cambodian. Got the report?"

"Got it somewheres."

He went to a file cabinet papered with photocopied notices on Commonwealth stationery, attached by magnets fashioned to resemble small wedges of cake and pie. He came up empty and hipped the drawer shut. He lifted his straw hat and fanned himself.

"Don't you use that?" I said, nodding at the computer on a table alongside his desk.

"Hasn't worked since the day they brung it in here."

"Isn't there a service contract?"

He shot me a dark look, resettled his lid and waddled toward the back area, tweezing the seat of his pants from between buttocks the size of sofa cushions. He edged sideways and disappeared into the maze of shelves.

I went around the counter to the computer. It was an IBM, with a coat of dust on the shell that told me it had been down as long as the Pilgrim nuclear plant. Experimentally I snapped the power switch and heard the circuits hum to life. I hit the monitor switch and the screen lit up.

LaRosa was back too soon to have gone far, moving with surprising grace for a man his size. He had a single sheet of paper in his hand. Seeing me poking keys, he frowned at me. I shrugged. "Seems to be running okay. You have any floppies around?"

"I didn't say it was broken—I said it hasn't worked. I haven't used it. Hardware is something I get at True Value. I want software and floppies, I go the Combat Zone."

I shut down the machine. Back on the authorized side of the counter I faced Al LaRosa, who had a hand on the sheet of paper so I could see only random words between his fingers. "Can I make a copy, or doesn't the copier work?" I said.

"It works. It takes money."

"I figured. How much?"

"Twenty."

He wasn't talking about two thin dimes. I dealt a pair of Hamiltons onto the counter and waited while he burned off a copy and brought it over to Checkpoint Charlie. We both let go at the same moment. The tens vanished among his fingers like a magic trick he had been perfecting for years. The copy was shiny and as gray as a March sky, but I saw Bhuntan Tran's name typed in reverse order in the correct space. I was eager to see what the rest of the report would say, but just then I had a craving for sunlight and real air.

The car was hot enough to fire ceramics in. I got the windows down and sat there and started to scan the death certificate. Under state law, every homicide and fatal accident victim was required to be declared so by a county medical examiner. Most of the M.E.'s came out of central casting, old docs who would show up at the scene in the middle of the night, with Tilt-Wheel in the Olds to get it over the potbelly. They'd come wheezing out and kneel beside the body, squinting against the smoke from the cancer stick spiked in the corner of their mouths and finally grunt, "He's dead," as if there were a question in anyone's mind. Generally, it was routine to do an autopsy. Tran had gotten one. I scanned until I got to the recap of the findings. Blood and urine had tested clean for drugs, as St. Onge had already told me.

Then other words grabbed hold.

> *Major trauma to occipital lobes by gunshots*
> *behind right and left ear. Both wrists show*
> *abrasion, as if bound prior to shooting. (No*
> *rope or handcuffs found at scene.)*

Parked there at hot noon, I felt a chill squiggle along my backbone. Lieutenant Nate Rosenheck's drawl came back to me: "Y'all notice anything else about the shooting?" Was this what he'd meant?

I realized now what details the police had determined to hold back—but these were more than tidbits. I was left with the sour afterthought that St. Onge had not given me much at all.

I tried to pick a shortcut back to I-93, but there aren't any anymore. Boston was like a corpse, with long worms of traffic crawling over it. It was three-thirty when I got back to the office. The lag made it two-thirty in Houston. Rosenheck was out, but someone else knew my name, and I silently lauded Rosenheck's efficiency.

"We checked that name you gave us," the other cop said. "How you pronounce it?"

I told him.

"Right. Khoy. The scoop is he lived in San Jose about two years—lived pretty good too. Fancy pad, car, duds. Evidently made his money selling jewelry and precious stones. He was married briefly and divorced. Local police say he had one prior for domestic violence and possession of cocaine, a few years before he moved there. He got three months suspended and a year parole. But he hasn't been heard from in six months, maybe longer. There's a stale outstanding on him for parole violation."

"You have a name or a phone number for his ex-wife?"

"You've got everything I have." He paused. "Could it be this Khoy's deceased?"

We mulled that long distance for a moment, then I thanked him for his help. I like to reward competence, which is getting as scarce in our society as a high school grad who can read. I was tempted to spill what I had learned from Tran's death report, but I figured I had better let the Lowell PD do it, officially. We said we'd be in touch.

Outside, the tar was gummy underfoot, even in the lengthening shadows, and the air was abroil with hovering blue fumes from the traffic. Lowell's clocks are still synchronized to the old shift whistles of the mills. Seven-thirty and four are when you can make better time on foot. I hiked down the street to my dyslexic printer and made a copy of a copy. Not that I doubted Ed St. Onge would mail one to Houston, but I wanted to be prepared. Back at the office I left the inner door open for circulation and settled at my desk with a book. I read some more on the Khmer Rouge, whose emblem had become a cairn of skulls. Under their theories of social reorganization, anyone who had ever been out of the country, possessed skills beyond planting rice, or wore glasses—and therefore probably read books—was suspect and often summarily shot. I could take only a chapter of that before I put the book down.

As I was sitting there, the knob of the outer door turned. I looked up to see a pretty, silver-haired woman come right in. She was checking her makeup in a compact mirror. Seeing me, she started; her finely plucked eyebrows rose in surprise, and she glanced around quickly. A blush spread over her cheeks—not a lot of one, just enough to be disarming. "Goodness!" she said.

"Not much to look at this time of day, I admit," I said, "but it's home."

She gave an embarrassed little shrug. "I beg your pardon. I wanted Attorney Meecham."

Ah. My neighbor down the hall. It was a reasonable error. Take away his Thomas McKnight lithos, oriental rugs, and electronic office amenities, and his suite was a mirror image of mine. "Some guys get all the luck."

"Are you an attorney?" the woman asked.

"I'm a poet," I said. " 'Linger a little, for thou art fair.' "

Her hair had a sheen that went with the bar of mellow sunlight on the wall behind her like a gold setting on an antique cameo. "Mr. Meecham is representing me," she volunteered.

"I'm sure he'll do his best."

"Divorce." She offered a game little smile I had to admire. She kept it up and I smiled back and we locked on for a span of a few slow seconds, then she backed out the door and closed it between us, and life went on with only her after-image in my mind and the tarrying spice of her perfume in the room. Forty-eight? Fifty? Working hard to keep it, and holding time to a pretty good draw. But it was a treadmill that kept speeding up on us all. I couldn't blame her for the try, though. It was why I did my miles along the river mornings, why people went to high school reunions and did the shag and the twist, why old soldiers got together to toast battles won and lost. It was the grab each of us made to get what we never would because the clock didn't run backwards, and that was the name of that tune.

The sun pattern on the walls had assumed a lower angle, and the light dimmed a little. The motes of dust stirred by the woman's entry and departure twirled slowly toward the floor. I put my mind back in the book before me and read three pages before my telephone rang.

13

۞۞۞۞۞۞۞۞

NIGHT HAD FALLEN. When I parked where I could see the spotlighted white-on-red sign—DRAGON RESTAURANT: THAI, LAO, CAMBODIAN, CHINESE, AND VIETNAMESE FOOD—and smell the aromas filling the hot dark, I realized I had not eaten dinner. Somehow, though, I didn't think Samol Lim would want to eat. On the phone he had said in *front* of the restaurant, and he had said after dark.

It was going on 9:05, just after the time we had agreed on. Lim's English had been simple and direct, better than his wife's whom he said had given him my card as I had asked her to. Lim had also seemed reluctant about meeting me.

As I waited, a Camaro cruised past with a big rumbly engine and chrome mags (and a quartet of Cro-Mags inside, yelling and tossing beer cans). I didn't figure they were looking for the city library. The driver stopped at the corner and red-lined the mill awhile before he popped the clutch. Burnt tire smoke overrode the food smells and hung in the air long after the banshee wail had faded. If the city would just organize these guys, for a few cases of Bud it could get the streets paved with fresh rubber.

By 9:15 I was starting to wonder if Lim had changed his

94

mind when I heard a soft tap at the passenger side door. I had seen no one appear on the street at all.

"You the policeman?" a young Asian man asked. He didn't have to stoop to peer in the window.

"Close enough. Samol Lim?"

"Yes."

He opened the door and slid in quickly, pulling the door closed. I keep the dome light turned off; when I'm sitting in the car at night I usually don't want to advertise it.

Lim was wiry, with a mop of black hair that made his head look too big for his shoulders. He had on sandals and jeans and a fishnet shirt that showed thin, tattooed arms. His face was coffee brown and private, and I imagined he was checking me out just as carefully as I was him. He had not showed up the way he had for no reason.

"Do you understand why I'm asking questions?" I said.

"You want to know who kill Bhuntan?"

"Yes, although that's for the official police. Someone has hired me to try to prove Tran wasn't doing bad things. Tell me, did Bhuntan take drugs?"

"He never take drug," said Lim with the certainty his wife had shown.

"But the police found cocaine at his house."

Lim wasn't dissuaded. His hair bounced like a symphony conductor's. "I was friend with Bhuntan since he come here. He was very good man, work very hard. He like to get married again, have children. He have bad memory of Cambodia, where all his family die."

"Did he have any enemies here?"

"Here, no enemy. In Cambodia, Khmer Rouge."

"Was he a member of a gang?"

"No gang."

"Why did he receive five thousand dollars from someone named Suoheang Khoy?"

Lim was slower answering. "I didn't know this until you say it to my wife and she say to me. Who is Suoheang Khoy?"

"I was hoping you could tell me. He was living in California two years ago when Tran was there."

His face seemed to show recognition. "Ah—Khoy maybe Bhuntan's friend in California who make money."

"Cambodian?"

"Yes."

"Did Tran tell you about him?"

"Only little. He sell jade and making much money."

"Jade—the precious stone?"

"Yes."

"Where did he get jade?"

Lim glanced outside and fell silent while a couple walked by. When they had passed he said, "In old Phnom Penh some people collect. Maybe he have it and keeping it with him. When Khmer Rouge take city, many citizen bury valuable in their garden so soldier not find. Some took valuable with them, or maybe buy rice. Cambodian money no good after Khmer Rouge come."

I knew it from my reading. Amounts of the Cambodian riel which once would have purchased a home might get a few pounds of rice. Anyone with gold watched it carefully, because only gold kept any value. And maybe jade?

"How did Tran know Suoheang Khoy?" I asked.

"Maybe met when Bhuntan first come to United State. Bhuntan arrive in California first. Come here after."

I asked a few more questions, but there was little to learn. I debated, then decided to tell Lim what I had learned from the M.E.'s report. He looked tough enough

96

to hear it. I told him about Tran's hands possibly having been bound, and about the gunshot pattern. In the dim reach of light from the Dragon Restaurant, I thought I saw the man's eyes change. Something passed across them like the shadow a raptor casts circling high over a small animal it's going to eat.

"Does that mean anything?" I asked.

Lim's jaw muscles bunched, and he angled his flat, lined face away. "Khmer Rouge get answer like this."

Not sure what he meant, I hesitated and he said it again, more forcefully, impatient with me. "Khmer Rouge get answer."

"When they interrogated someone?"

It was his turn to be puzzled. I thought of words to re-phrase it, but the gestures are universal: seize an imagi-nary shirt front, slash a hand across a face. Lim nodded grimly and put a finger pistol behind his right ear, then did the same with the left. I felt a chill. It was an execution method used by the Khmer Rouge.

Lim said, "I friend with Bhuntan. He was brave man. But when I talk to him last time, he's seem . . . sca-red."

There it was again—two syllables this time, but the same word Cassie Samms had used. "Scared of what?"

Lim was rubbing his hands over the fading tattoos on his slim, muscled arms. "Don't know."

I noticed something in my side mirror. As casually as I could, so as not to spook him more than he already seemed to be, I said to Samol Lim, "Let's ride a little, okay?"

He frowned a question at me.

"Just ride," I said.

I started the car and eased away from the curb and drove slowly to the intersection where I made a left onto

Market Street, past the Rendezvous Dine and Dance, a holdover from the 1930s, where in more recent memory a patron had pulled life at Walpole for the castration killing of his wife's lover. We headed back downtown, over the trolley tracks and cobblestones. The wide-set headlights of the car I had noticed stayed a few cars back in the evening traffic. I swung left onto Gorham and again onto Merrimack. Taking the drag slow enough to catch some of the traffic lights, I meandered back toward the Acre.

"Do you have any friends who drive a big car?" I asked Lim. "Maybe a Cadillac?"

He got my meaning and glanced rearward. He seemed a little flustered, as if he should have refused my request to meet, because now something he had been dreading was finally coming to pass. But he shook his head and faced front again.

There was still the possibility of coincidence, I supposed, so I pulled in front of the police station and stopped. The tail car slowed in momentary hesitation, then drove past. I saw the silhouette of a driver in a two-tone green Lincoln Town Car as long as a mortgage.

I hooked an illegal U and headed back into the Acre. "I'll let you out anywhere you say."

He gave me an intent glance. "You got bad trouble? I stay with you."

"No need," I said. "In fact, if I drop you here instead of at your door, it'll be safer for you. In case anyone is still looking."

He got out but left one arm on the door. "Good luck, mister," he said.

He flitted away as swiftly as he had appeared. The citizens had told him he was not particularly welcome; that he had too many kids, that his food stank of fish, and his language was just a harsh noise. I liked him. He was a brave man determined to survive in this new world.

I circumnavigated several blocks then drove back to the office. I eased into the lot and stowed the car behind Lenzi's Catering and S & N Cab. As I shut off the motor I automatically scanned what I could see of the lot behind me in the rearview. A few weak bulbs mounted on the building wall painted the rutted pavement and old brick with splotchy light. But it was enough.

Inconspicuous as the *QE II* at a fish pier, the Lincoln was backed into a fence that bordered the canal. I thought I could make out the shadowed driver behind the steering wheel. There was no front tag to be seen, which meant the car was Mass-registered. I considered getting out of there, betting that the Bobcat could smoke the big car in the downtown maze. I didn't move. Whoever it was back there was patient. He had returned here on the chance that I would too. He would catch up sooner or later.

Taking it slow, as if I had not seen a thing, I climbed out. My hand wanted to shake a little as I poked the key into the slot and locked the door. My shadow fell across the asphalt as big as I wished I were. Juiced with adrenaline, I turned and bolted toward the Lincoln.

The driver had been lulled for a few seconds, but now he shoved open his door, and I saw the big sloping head, the heavy shoulders as he turned to climb out, and I made the call.

I hit his door flat-palmed and shoved it back, jamming him in. The fist he threw over the top of the open window frame had iron in it and struck sparks as it skated across my skull. The interior lights strobed with the uncertain forces on either side of the door, and I had only a winking impression of the man's face, but it was enough. I got a dizzy sensation of peering back through the mists of time. The man was brutish and jut-jawed, with a thatch of dark hair over an inch-high forehead, beneath which glinted tiny eyes as cold as stones.

That was all the character study I had time for. Someone was behind me. I swung around to see who, but what I saw instead was a blaze of light, as if a flashbulb had gone off in my eyes. Then the rutted alley rose to meet me.

14

⊘⊘⊘⊘⊘⊘⊘

GROGGILY I BLINKED the world into focus. I was in the back seat of the Lincoln, going east on 133. The courtesy lights in the doors were on. The caveman was at the wheel. The little guy who owned the last face I remember seeing sat in the back with me, a block away in the opposite corner. He had on a wideshouldered sportcoat with lapels you could hide a violin behind. He had a mashed beak and shiny scar tissue at the hairline. He hadn't gotten that face sitting in an office. A name started coming to me now—Oscar something. Not de la Renta. He had been a jockey. I thought I knew something else too, but I could not snatch it.

My headache was up around eight on the Excedrin scale. I fingered the back of my skull to see if any gray matter had oozed out, but surprisingly there was only a small bump.

"Hey, you started the hand jive," Oscar said. His voice was a gnarly sound, like chicken bones in a Disposall. With a face and clothes like that, what did I expect? "If you'da been at your crib or your office in the first place, none of this woulda happened."

Not Handlin, either, or the little gold guy they handed out in Hollywood.

101

"But you weren't either place, so we said the hell with it. We was goin' for a drink, when I spot your shitbox in front of the gook joint. You got cute by the cop station, yeah, but I figured you'd show back at your office—beats spendin' time in that dump you live in."

"Him I saw," I said, nodding at the driver. "Where were you?"

He grinned. "Drainin' the dragon. Lucky for you. He woulda used his fists, not a sap."

I knew where the pain without the big knot had come from. Maybe I had got the better deal at that. The guy hunched at the wheel gave me serious doubts about human evolution. Hair thatched down his neck into his shirt. I could not see much face in the rearview except for a rectangle of reflected light that lay across it like an inverse burglar's mask. I remembered the B.C. brow and the stony eyes. He drove the Lincoln with mitts clamped at ten and two on the wheel, never moving them, tilting his whole torso left or right when he made a turn. He didn't have to make many. We kept on 133. I tried to grab the other thing Oscar reminded me of, but couldn't.

"Well," I said, shifting position to get more comfortable, "the night's young. Where to?"

Oscar pinched at his nose and looked out.

"Not even a hint?"

Silence.

"You still a member of the horsey set?" I asked.

It was the one-sided conversation dentists get good at. I didn't mind; it kept my mind off the pain enveloping it.

"I'm only going to say this once," I said, "I don't fool around on the first date."

Oscar turned to me. "Shut it."

After awhile we crossed I-93 and passed the Sheraton

Rolling Green hotel, and soon B.C. slowed the Lincoln and bulldogged it left onto a road that went through moonlit woods for a half mile before it opened into meadow. A shimmer of mist hung over the high grass, and fireflies winked in it. The road was a cul-de-sac, empty except for a single large house which sat on a turnaround at the end. It was of a modern design, jutting and glassy, ringed with small ground-lights which, in the kilowatt glow flooding out from the house, seemed redundant.

We pulled into a driveway. Just before B.C. killed the headlights, I saw a three-bay garage at the end. In the middle drive, as distinctly sleek as a hundred-thousand-dollar Dumpster, sat a royal blue Rolls. That's what reminded me of what I had forgotten before . . . and told me where we were.

Oscar motioned me out. We walked up a flagstone path toward the house. It was certainly a different piece of heaven than any I had been in lately. The air bore the spice of roses, and except for the *snitch* of sprinklers showering a side lawn, the only sound was the *whip-poor-will* of a nighthawk.

My guide opened the front door of the house, and we stepped into a broad atrium with a gleaming marble floor. Whole trees grew out of copper planters you could have cooked missionaries in.

"It's not much," I said, "but it's home."

Oscar led me across the foyer to a room at the left. It was lit by little spots washing over large, gilt-framed paintings that would have been old when Whistler was still playing at his mother's knee. They made a nice contrast with the modernity evident everywhere else—like the entertainment center hogging the wall we had come through. I would not have blinked to see a chorus line come legging out, waving top hats and singing. Instead, a glass door at the back slid open and Joel Castle stepped in.

He was in a Speedo swimsuit, a towel slung around his neck, his muscular chest pebbled with droplets of water. His hair was wet, and in the muted light it sprang in little corkscrews from his head like brass shavings.

"What took you?" he asked Oscar.

"He wasn't in the first time, Mr. C. So what happens? We spot him, right? We wanna talk. Next thing you know, he gets cute, we hadda tag him—but he started it."

Castle frowned. Stepping past Oscar with no further acknowledgment, he looked at me with concern. "Are you all right?"

"Never better. In a dark alley," I said, "some guy who looks like he takes heartworm pills comes at you, you don't stand around exchanging business cards."

Now he gave me the frown, then turned to his man. "Get out. I'll talk to you later." Oscar left as quietly as a cat. "I apologize for that," Castle said. "Sit down. Drink?"

"Water."

He raised his eyebrows.

"Perrier then." When someone else is buying, go top shelf.

At the gadget wall he poked buttons, and piano music began issuing into the room, as cool and soft as meadow mist. Bill Evans, if I had to guess. I found my way into an armchair of chrome and nubbled gray fabric, before which was a low table spread with copies of *GQ* and *Antiques*. Castle tonged rocks into a pair of crystal glasses, poured sparkling water into one and scotch into the other. Cutty Sark. He handed me the water. I wondered if Lauren was here in the house, but somehow I knew she wasn't. "Long while," Castle said. "Cheerios."

"Wheaties."

It *had* been a long while. I had not remembered that toast until just that moment. The last time we used it we had been sitting in a graveyard drinking Harvard Ale, too young to be drinking it in a bar.

"I'll be right back," Castle said and went out.

Joel Castle and I had known each other in that long-ago fifteenth summer that screenwriters envision in perpetual soft focus. Ours was a grittier light, that of old Lowell, and we were just hanging out and just avoiding trouble. He was Joey Costello then, with a dentist for an old man and more pocket money than the families of the rest of us had in the bank combined. And money was where he got his ideas: cruising up to Hampton Beach in his dad's Eldy ragtop and paying some stewbum to buy the beer, or to Mass. Ave. in Roxbury where the hookers on the street corner fooled with us, knowing we were just kids wasting their time and ours. But time was something we'd had a lot of then.

When we hit high school, his new friends were people I did not need to know, people for whom kicks was whiskey and the first marijuana I'd ever heard of. We drifted apart, and a few years later, while Costello was pledging Kappa Sig, I was invited to Uncle Sam's G.I. party. Joey beat the draft the same way Joe Namath had: with knees you could only play football on.

Later I found out that higher ed had lasted only two terms before he was out the door, on the streets, bouncing. Always his old man's net was there though, to catch him when he bounced too far. In the end, having had the luxury of being a screwup ten years longer than most people, he settled into legitimacy. He took his patrimony in a lump sum. The name got changed to Castle, now appearing on marquees all over eastern Mass as Castle Cleen

Dry Cleaners, in by nine, out by five, all work guaranteed
*spotless. It had worked for him. Now his friends were con-
gressmen and Boston TV personalities and pro athletes.
Not gumshoes working out of their hats. I hadn't had a
drink with him in a lot of years. The Harvard brewery had
turned belly up two decades ago, and now time was something he measured on the slim gold Daniel Mink watch on
his tanned wrist.

"Better get to it," I said when he reappeared, freshened
and wearing a silk robe in the same blue as the Rolls outside. "Nostalgia only goes so far."

"Still the joker." But he didn't smile. "I spoke with
Lauren today. She was pretty upset by the conversation
you two had the other evening."

"She seemed pretty happy through most of it."

He sat opposite me. "It was her idea to see you. I figure
you're owed no special treatment. All's fair. But she insisted on telling you." His shoulders rose and fell under
the blue silk. "I'm happy when she's happy."

"Two out of three ain't bad."

"I wanted us to talk."

"Something wrong with the telephone?"

"I don't like dealing with people's tape machines.
They're dehumanizing."

"I was thinking something like that about B.C. and
Oscar."

"They're my chauffeur and my personal assistant."

"That's like calling brass knuckles a gum massager."

Joey frowned. "He used brass knuckles?"

"A sap."

That relieved him a little. Possession of knucks is higher
on the crime scale; my head did not make the distinction,
though.

"That's the difference between an ex-jockey and an ex-boxer," he said.

"And here I thought it had something to do with their shorts."

Castle wasn't amused. "They were only supposed to pick you up. I apologized already. Are you going to press charges?"

I made a sour face and he nodded thanks. "Anyway, we're not here to discuss me or my employees. It's Lauren I'm concerned with, and in spite of it all, I think you are too."

I swallowed fizzy water from cut crystal. In the dark meadow beyond the glass walls, fireflies glowed, or maybe it was the reflection of LEDs from all the hi-fi gear. "I guess I don't get something," I said, setting the glass down on Jeff Goldblum's face on the cover of *GQ*.

"What's that?"

"Beyond the obvious—why Lauren?" I slid my gaze around the big room, the bolted beam ceiling, the accent-lighted paintings, the carpets, back to the diamond chips that caught the light and winked like stars in the little gold planetarium on his wrist. "Why not a starlet, or a model, some lollipop who fits the picture you've painted yourself into?"

He said, "You don't get it, do you."

"Clue me, I'm slow."

His brown eyes, which had stayed as cool as coat buttons, took the room tour like mine just had. "I've been there," he said. "That stuff's fantasy. I want for real."

What was I going to say? That Lauren wasn't?

"When I met her," he said, "it was a New Year's Eve dinner party, a quiet evening. She was down. The hostess is a mutual friend, thought people might cheer Lauren. It didn't work."

I could credit what he was saying. Lauren and I had talked before the holidays, so I knew she was feeling the split. There was no Santa Claus for either of us last winter, but she insisted that we keep it that way.

Castle said, "I guess at first it was a challenge to try to get her out of her depression. Not just that, that sounds impersonal. Obviously I was attracted to her. She's beautiful. We talked several times on the phone, finally she consented to meet me for dinner. She wasn't impressed. I knew that first night I'd never have to buy her."

"You couldn't," I said.

He nodded. "I'm tired of women who if you drove up in a Ford wouldn't give you the time of day, but they see a big car, they're pulling your fly down." He tasted his scotch. "Anyway, it was all on the up and up, and as winter started to fade, her spirits began to lift. I don't know that it was even me. It was just a good feeling to be with her as she came back up. I'd never really felt that . . . empathy before. I'm a late learner, Alex, you know that."

I peered at Jeff Goldblum through the bottom of the glass. He looked good with a monocle. "Maybe we both are," I said.

"Anyway, by then I'd fallen in love with her."

"Even though she was still married."

"Wake up, Rasmussen. I know how things stand." He waved a hand. "There was no bullshit. It happened. For her too."

I had to take that one. Lauren *had* changed: she was happier.

"Now I'm ready," Castle said. "For what everyone else has had right along, I'm ready." He drained his glass and, ignoring the cork coaster, set it on the table with a clack. I hoped it would leave a ring. He said, "I don't want to see her caught in the middle of anything ugly."

Though I had done a lot of it in my time, I still hated losing. "What if I said no to her?"

"Maybe I'd try to persuade you to say yes."

"Send along the tag team?"

"How about an offer of something you could use."

He had brass, I had to give him that. It was hard not to like Castle, golden boy that he was, but I had a pretty good head start, and an ache in the back of my neck that was trying to root down to my feet. I stood up. "You can hang onto your checkbook. The papers are already in the works."

He rose too. His hair had dried in little licks and points like a laurel wreath cast in bronze. "Would you care for a real drink—a nightcap?"

Just like that. Business taken care of, we were friends now. A half-dozen smart remarks turned to sand on my tongue. "A ride to the city will do."

The chauffeur took me. The silence all the way back to Lowell was welcome.

15

⟨⟨⟨⟨⟨⟨⟨⟨⟨

IT WAS LATE to be at the office, but I was not going to sleep for awhile. I adjusted the gooseneck lamp. Using the edge of the desk, I tore several sheets of paper into quarters. The desk was good for that. It had belonged to the Army recruiter across the street. I used to see him standing in there behind the posters in his dress greens, looking out through the plate glass in the wistful way barbers used to in the sixties. Then the Rambo-Ronbo duo made war glamorous again and suddenly every lonely kid who had ever mooned over the Daisy air rifles on the backs of comic books and felt he had something to prove joined up. The government took an old aircraft carrier out of mothballs for the recruiter's new desk, and I bought this and the three-drawer file cabinet as a twofer, both the wishful brain-gray that's big in public offices. It was right for this office too. And a good straight-edge to boot.

A different man would have been in Atlanta right then, or Tampa, or Tombstone, working on the foundation of a new life with his family. He'd be using the late hour to address envelopes so he could get his résumé off in the morning's mail to headhunters and human resource managers. Finally he would tiptoe in to peer at his sleeping babes before kissing his wife good night and snuggling up in the darkness, hanging on in that posture which is like a fetal curl, praying there were no hairline cracks in the foundation.

I took my paper slips and began to write bits of what I knew about the Tran case on each one. It was a lot briefer task than writing what I didn't know. I dealt them into small piles by category across the naked desktop.

Sometimes making lists works, or free-associating into a tape recorder. Occasionally I get an idea while I'm sweating out a five-mile run. Tonight I played solitaire. For suits I had: Tran as seen by others; details of the murder; Tran's jobs; the person the Azar woman saw crossing Tran's yard; drugs.

On another slip of paper I wrote: "Suoheang Khoy."

I gathered the hands and reshuffled them, added a few cards and dealt again.

The murder details pile was both the biggest and the easiest to put aside. Since the police investigation was ongoing, physical evidence was their domain. It was possible they had held out on me in other ways, and I had no way of knowing that. Likewise, the piles relating to Tran's jobs and acquaintances were not tricky. He had been a hard worker and was, by most accounts, amiable and competent.

The short piles were tougher. Like "drugs"—I still had no definite feel for that one. Or for the person Claire Azar had seen emerge from the woods on the night before the murder. Was that why Cassie Samms had described Tran as seeming scared that next day? Had someone come to tell him something? Or threaten him?

Which brought me to the last pile.

Suoheang Khoy had given Tran five thousand dollars

two years ago. Khoy had dealt in jade and made money and spent it on a good time. Khoy had jumped parole and disappeared from San Jose six months ago, around the time that several other Cambodians had been murdered out there. Maybe Khoy was dead too. Or maybe not. I slid the pile closer to the Azar card and asked myself the obvious questions.

It was after eleven-thirty, but I took a chance. The desk officer put the call through.

"St. Onge," said the weary voice.

"Still polishing pine?"

I sensed his one instant of indecision over whether to hang up. Encouraging obscene callers can be a mistake. "I should be out in the streets where the bad guys are," he said.

"Not all of them."

"That's cryptic."

"I saw the coroner's report on the Tran shooting."

He was quiet a moment, maybe wishing he had hung up. "I wasn't at liberty to spill much."

"Why bother at all?"

"What, were you going to solve it?" he said with sudden heat. "For crissakes, I told you it looked like a hit. How'd you run this call past the desk anyway?"

"You're talking to Louis L'Amour."

"Swell. Stick both our necks in the wringer."

"Relax, in this town what's another Frenchman. I've got a question for you."

"Forget it. I'm hanging up. Go on home. What?"

"Play with a name for me."

"Why should I?"

"You decide. Suoheang Khoy."

"The guy in your report. No bells."

"I know you're a one-man anti-crime force, but could you check a file? One of your worthy colleagues might've turned him up around town lately."

"Who is he anyway?"

"A blip that keeps appearing on radar. Maybe no one."

"Rasmussen, it's late."

"Then why aren't you home with your family?"

He sighed. "He have an address?"

"Last known was San Jose."

"California? Then what the hell you asking me—?"

"He faded from there six months ago. He could be moving around. He could've come here, Ed." I did not mention that he also could be dead.

Another sigh; but he did not hang up. I heard footsteps wander off. He was gone so long that I half-imagined he had asked the way to San Jose and gone in person, that his voice would have turned to a croak with the Silicon Valley smog and the passage of time.

It hadn't. "Negative," he said.

"You checked drug arrests?"

"I checked overdue *library* books! The name draws nothing. You done now?"

This time *I* sighed. "Yeah." The fact was, if Khoy had come east, he probably would have changed his name to some other, equally unpronounceable name. Why the hell hadn't these people stayed where they belonged? I told him about the Houston's PD's request, and he agreed to send them his report.

"We square now?" he asked.

"Even Steven."

"Then I'll throw in a bonus, no charge. What does this make it for you and the Stewart woman? Three days?"

"You seem to be keeping track."

113

"It could be you've done your duty by her and should collect your fee."

"Meaning?"

"That's a pretty good piece of change. Take it. She's not going to want to go on shelling out for nothing. I'll handle things from here."

"I thought you'd been trying all along."

"Look at it from another angle. All this grand jury stuff over at city hall has got Droney acting crazy."

"That's new?"

"It's no joke. He's looking for a dog to kick. He hasn't forgotten the run-in you two had. He finds out you're nosing around a police case . . ."

"You're saying I should butt out while I can."

"And?"

"Pearls before swine," I said. "Let me elaborate on that. No. Negative. *Nyet.* I'm the one who decides when I work and when I don't. I haven't got a gold tie-bar and a pension waiting for me at the end, which also means nobody but my client tells me when to pull the plug on a job. All things considered, I like the trade just fine."

I hung up the phone. For a moment I sat there with the tremblies. I realized I had been looking for a free midnight snack; instead I had gotten indigestion.

When you're losing at solitaire, you can cheat or pack it in. I gathered the slips of paper, clamped them with a paper clip, slid the deck into my coat pocket and locked up. The elevator had been fixed, but it grumbled all the way down like I had wakened it from a sweet dream. The streets were mostly quiet—a distant gunning car, the hoot of a freight train. A patrolman was rattling doorknobs on Merrimack. The facade of the *Sun* building was splashed with milky light from a chipped cup of a moon. The air had finally cooled. I walked around to the lot in back of my building with an alert eye. I had not forgotten what had happened there earlier.

A scrap of paper was pinned under one of my wiper blades.

Alex—I saw your car and stopped by, but you weren't upstairs. Call me tomorrow? —Ada.
P.S. Had fun last night.

It was an unexpectedly nice cap to the day. I took the pack of notes out of my pocket and slipped Ada's note on the bottom. Maybe for luck.

16

ᘒᘒᘒᘒᘒᘒᘒᘒᘒ

EVERYTHING ABOUT THE reception-
ist at the DSS office was fire-truck red, from the frames of
her oversized glasses to the rim of lipstick on her morning
cup of coffee—even the fresh-looking sunburn across her
cheeks and forehead. In Tailgunner Joe's day, she would
have been a definite question mark. Her smile was white
and friendly, though, as she pointed me toward the cubicles at the back of the large bullpen. I made my way past a
lot of harried-looking people with phones hooked to their
ears. Ada was just hanging hers up when I peered through
her open doorway.

"Knock, knock," I said.

"Oh, hi," she said, surprised. "Come in."

She touched her hair, smoothed her skirt as I settled
into a wooden folding chair.

"Thanks for your note last night," I said. "I didn't get
back until late."

"I was in the area. How's the investigation coming?"

"TGIF."

"No luck?"

"There's a little smoke but no fire. You're not paying
me to give you a bunch of questions."

"You'll answer them."

116

"I like your confidence."

"It's not misplaced, is it?"

"If I thought so I'd collect my security deposit and get a job in a shoe store. I'm just not sure the answers are going to warrant the cost."

"Alex"— she glanced past me to the door and back —"have you got a minute?"

"Loads of them, one right after another."

She led me into a passageway between more cubicles toward a rear door. Walt Rittle was in a rat-hole at the end, scanning a computer screen. As we passed he looked up and I waved.

"Hey, how you doing?" His greeting had its hearty ring.

Ada indicated the door. Humidity had swollen it, so I had to butt it open with my shoulder. I did not shut it tight behind us, for fear we wouldn't get back in. In the little paved parking lot sunlight shone off windshields and chrome.

"If we could bottle Walter's energy, we'd have something," Ada said, leading the way over to her little Toyota. Bumper stickers said TAKE BACK THE NIGHT and EXTINCT IS FOREVER. "He's the only social worker I know who's lasted in the trenches past forty. He puts us younger folks to shame."

"You do okay," I said.

"Just barely." Ada leaned against her car and tipped her head back, closing her eyes. In the brightness I could see tiny lines at the corners, like delicate Chinese fans. Her hair gleamed the deep burnished brown of teak.

"The sun is tonic," she said, her eyes still shut. "Weekends I just sit on the deck at home, reading."

"State reports, no doubt."

Her faint smile was a confession.

"Why not take a week and do it right?" I said. "Go to the Cape."

"There's too much work."

I clicked my tongue. "The little Dutch kid disease is in its terminal phase."

She opened her eyes. "We had this conversation. Anyway, that's not why I got you out here. In 1859 my great-grandfather went shares in a clipper ship, which meant that he'd get that portion of any profit. Before long he had six ships of his own operating out of Salem. He took cotton cloth to Canton and Shanghai and brought back tea and ceramics and silk tapestries. Eventually he brought back some people, whom he paid to work as servants. To make a long story short, they had children, and one of the little girls married the old man's grandson, Charles Blaine Stewart the Third. They were my mother and father."

"I wondered about that."

"They've been divorced since I was thirteen. He lives in Europe most of the year, she's in Palm Beach. My brother and I are the heirs. I live on the salary I make working, but there's money in trust. A lot of it, Alex." She hesitated. "Something like four million dollars."

She turned away abruptly, as if she had confessed to an unsavory disease. It would have been a nice affliction to have, but it was an affliction all the same. I said, "It's still a matter of value for your money. I've got to be satisfied I'm giving you that."

"I understand. I'm telling you this only so you'll know. No one else around here does. Some people can't relate to the notion of working if you don't have to. Do I need to explain it to you?"

I smiled. "No, though I don't speak from experience."

She gave another grin. The sudden bugling of a horn drew our attention across the street, where a canteen truck drew up in front of an auto repair shop. The driver got out and hoisted the quilted stainless steel back. Workers began to emerge from the gloom of the garage wiping their hands on orange cloths.

"Want something?" I said. "I'm spending."

I went over and got a hot dog and a pair of coffees and brought them back. "For lunch?" Ada said skeptically as I unwrapped the foil on the hot dog.

"Breakfast," I said. "You are what you eat."

She watched me squeeze on mustard and relish, then said, "So where are we?"

"Right where we were five minutes ago, I guess. With lots of questions. Here's another. Does your family know anything about jade?"

"Seriously?"

I nodded, chewing.

"Jade." She said the word softly. "The stone of heaven. That's what the Chinese have called it for centuries. They valued it more than gold. My great-grandfather's collection was one of the finest in America. Why?"

I shrugged. "Professional curiosity. Is there anyone in your family I could talk to about jade?"

"Most of the collection was sold or donated to museums long ago. Latter generations of Stewarts have opted for less beautiful but more practical forms of wealth. You really want to know more?"

"Yes."

"Well . . . the gallery my family used to deal with is still in Andover. Very old and prestigious. Haskell and MacKay, on Main Street. Angus MacKay knew jade better than anyone."

I wiped my fingers, got out my notebook and wrote the name.

"But he died years ago," Ada said.

I lined out the name.

"The people who run the gallery now are snobs, but they're still among the best art and antique brokers around. They could tell you what you want to know."

I put my notepad away. "It's a place to start."

"So you're still retained?"

"With all that money to play with?"

She grinned. "I've got to get back. Could I see you tonight? To find out how it's going?"

"I'll drop by here."

"Look for you about six-thirty?"

"Quitting early for a change?"

"TGIF." She wrinkled her nose. "Thanks for the coffee."

I drove downtown and checked in at my office. People weren't lined up ten deep for my services. Fred Meecham heard me and came by with the papers for the divorce. I got them signed and sealed and headed across the street to the post office, but when I was halfway there they started to grow heavy. I envisioned the envelope dropping through the slot and causing damage, which would get me a federal rap. I decided to deliver the papers in person before they got so heavy I needed a dump truck.

The house that Lauren and the bank and I still owned jointly was in the Highlands. A landscaping service was at work in the yard of a former neighbor: one shirtless young man with a mower decapitating dandelions as another whacked weeds by the fence encircling a new in-ground pool. Across the street another neighbor was strapping toddlers into safety seats in a Volvo where for years had stood a yellow AMC Hornet with freckles of rust showing through like a banana going bad. The neighborhood had slipped a few notes up the scale without me.

I parked in front of our pale gray colonial, climbed the steps and rang the bell. Lauren's green Accord was in the driveway. I could smell the tea roses trained on trellises to either side. The stoop was neatly swept and the welcome mat was new. I squinted up at the gutter and downspouts, at the glazing on the windows, looking for the little signs of neglect that would demand a man's touch, but there were none that I could see. Someone was getting along just fine.

My knock brought no hurrying footsteps, nor slow ones either. The mail had already come. It was in the box. I held the fat envelope in my hand a moment, then slipped it through the slot. It hit bottom with a thud—or was that my stomach? As I walked back to the car, I did feel lighter, but it was a hollow lightness, the kind you get at the top of the roller coaster just before the plummet. I drove off wondering whether I would ever come here again.

If I had known then what I was still several hours away from knowing, I never would have left.

17

⚈⚈⚈⚈⚈⚈

ANDOVER, TWICE IN as many days: my star was on the rise. I stowed the car in a town lot behind the stores in the center, coined the meter and strolled over to Main Street, where I had to wade through folks in Eddie Bauer garb licking designer ice cream cones, and kids with first names like Kit and Potter and Abigail, with time on their hands between oboe lessons, computer camp, and growing up to inherit the portfolio.

Haskell and MacKay was tucked at the end of a block of shops with striped awnings and hand-carved wooden signs with gold lettering. Everything matched and was bright as a new penny. When you stepped through the door of the gallery, however, a hush descended on you, and the new Andover ended right there. Inside was the Andover of Phillips Academy and two-hundred-year-old Congregational churches and the DAR. Listening carefully, I thought I could hear money being minted behind folding Oriental screens that decorated one wall.

When my vision had adjusted to the cool dimness, I saw a woman standing in profile at the far end of a Bokhara carpet the size of a badminton court. She was leaning against a table with a Tiffany lamp on it and a French telephone, the receiver of which was cupped to her ear and into whose mouthpiece she was quietly speaking. She had one long leg knee-locked and taking her weight while the other foot was rolled over on its side, doing a demure striptease with a navy blue pump. Some signal bell must have jingled, because she looked around with fleeting appraisal and held up a finger—one minute—that rooted me to the spot.

I busied myself checking out some small paintings hanging on a side wall. Mostly they were as old and dark as a Dutch master, so you had to peer close to see what was going on. I saw cows grazing along a stream bank; two Gordon setters in a meadow; a creel with a brace of brook trout laid beside it. There wasn't a price tag in sight.

The painting that held my eye was a gold-framed affair showing a group of men in black robes and white periwigs, standing around looking sober.

"It's English," said the woman, "circa 1835."

I hadn't heard her cradle the phone.

She started over. Both her shoes were on now and she moved easily on the long legs in a paisley silk dress that had been built to show off the great figure.

"Barristers and judges," she went on. "I've always liked the formality of the costumes. It makes the law seem very strict and certain, don't you think?"

"If the judges over here wore costumes," I said, "they'd be red suits with big white beards."

Her hair was center-parted, just off the shoulder and of the rich brown that would go well with the mahogany mantel of one of the big homes on Main Street, and the rich amber of old brandy, and money that never has to turn green because it is all long certificates of paper in security drawers in Boston banks. She could have sent bone structure in care packages to modeling schools. Her

cheeks tapered smoothly to a firm jaw. She had apprais-
ing, river-blue eyes, a spray of tiny freckles across her
straight nose, and a full-lipped mouth.

"Do you like it?" she asked.

"Certainly pleasing to the eye," I said, my gaze still on
her. "Composition looks good."

She measured me with that cool stare. She had all the
candy and I was a kid holding out my trick-or-treat bag.
She said, "It's terribly expensive, though."

"Oh, I can imagine. But I'm just kicking tires. I'm
mainly here to ask about jade. Ada Stewart recommended
you people."

"Ada Stewart," she said, as if she had come across an
artifact in an attic. "Now there's a name to conjure with.
Poor Ada. We were at Miss Hall's School together."

I could have said most anything. "How nice for Miss
Hall," is what came out.

She didn't lose her place at the head of the line. "Ada
needed to feel *engagée*. Always the little rebel in those days,
trying to politicize everyone, writing essays in the school
paper, marching. She had 'Chan' legally put in her name.
Her parents didn't do that."

"It was a family name on her mother's side," I said.

She wasn't going to argue against old family names.
"Isn't Ada working in a ghetto now or something? Instead
of assuming the duties of the Blaine Stewart fortune? We
used to play in that huge family place when we were small.
Ada was always climbing the beech trees like a little mon-
key, and one of the Oriental servants was forever trying to
coax her down." She shook her head and gave a tiny
smile. "Ah, well. Jade, you said. Do you know anything
about jade?"

"It's green."

124

One corner of her mouth curled. "When it isn't white or lavender or black or some other color. Come over to the desk."

I got settled in a chair that might have been Chippendale or Sheraton; hell, maybe it was Danish Modern. She excused herself and went through an open doorway into the back. I took a business card from a little bone china basket and learned the proprietors were Dayle Haskell and Syd Keyes. Those damn cute names that drove you to that hoary old greeting on business letters: "Dear Sir or Madame." The woman returned with two books and set them before me and leaned over my shoulder to give me a glimpse of the jewels. I drew my attention back to the books. She opened the first one, and I saw color photographs set behind clear plastic.

"For over fifty centuries jade was the traditional heart of Chinese civilization. It was prized more than gold even, or other gemstones. And it's harder than steel, so it was used for tools and weapons." She slowly turned pages as she spoke. "But it was also prominent in art and religion. Among members of the imperial court, a finely carved piece of jade could be worth more than life itself."

She turned to a photograph of a carving in the shape of a large insect. It was the color of paraffin wax. "In fact," she said, "jade was considered a bridge to immortality."

"That's jade?" I asked.

"Yes. It's a cicada. At death, one of these would be put in the mouth of the deceased, as a totem of reincarnation."

I remembered Ada had called jade the stone of heaven.

The woman opened the second volume. "These depict pieces that were in the Blaine Stewart collection."

Between the plastic pages were photographs of small

jade disks with holes cut in the center, which she said were called *pi,* used in burial rites. There were also carved animals and human figurines, necklaces, amulets.

"This mask was worn by a Chinese warlord centuries ago. It's currently owned by Duncan MacGregor, of the meat packing fortune."

I marveled at the variety and delicate beauty of the work. Ada's forebears had been into something mesmerizing. But everything the woman showed me was old, and I said so.

"Oh, jade is popular still," she said, "though much of what passes for it is imitation. There is some fine new carving being done in a few scattered places, but most of the truly classic work, the old stuff, has long since been secured by private collections and museums."

"Is white more valuable than green?"

"That color is called 'mutton fat.' Depends. Black is probably the most costly jade, gram for gram, because it's the most rare. But color is only one consideration. What we call jade really refers to two stones—jadeite and nephrite." She gave me her half-inch smile. "Is this getting too technical?"

"I'll say when."

"The bright green you're likely to see on the market is typically jadeite. Mostly it comes raw from the old Burma, and some gets sold on the market there, but under the Communists the prices are fixed, so a lot gets smuggled out through Thailand into China and Hong Kong and Taiwan. Among connoisseurs, the old Chinese nephrite is the most prized."

"Is it collected in Southeast Asia?"

"When the French were there, absolutely. The colonial economy encouraged collecting of all kinds among the well-to-do Indo-Chinese. These days I doubt it. In that part of the world everyone's just poor now, aren't they?" She closed the book.

I thanked her for her help and held up the business card and used my superior deductive skills. "Dayle?"

"Sydney Keyes."

"That's what I meant."

She was studying me again, as if I was going on the auction block soon. "Coincidentally," she said, "one of our customers recently purchased some Yunung-kash."

"What's Yunung-kash?" I said.

"It's very valuable old nephrite jade. The original boulders it was carved from were brought by caravan from the Yunung-kash, which is a river in a remote oasis in the Takla Makan Desert in China."

"Oh, *that* Yunung-kash," I said. "When did you sell it?"

"We didn't. It was acquired in a private sale. But that's what made me think of it. I believe the seller was Indo-Chinese."

"Do you have a name?"

"No. But we did an appraisal for the individual who bought the jade. Seven pieces dating from the late Ming and early Qing periods. You are familiar with the dynasties?"

"They're both on my all-time list," I said. "You mind if I ask the buyer's name?"

"Ordinarily, yes, I would mind. However, since mention of the purchase has already appeared in the newspaper, it's a well-leaked secret. It was Joel Castle."

"Of the Castle Cleen fortune?"

She gave me the tiny smile, which I understood now meant amusement. "Are you planning to become a collector, Mr. Rasmussen?"

127

"Who's got the time? My other collections keep me tapped out."

A delicate skepticism arched her brows. "Really?"

"For years now. Come out to the car, I'll show you my parking tickets." I thanked her again for her help.

"I'm here Monday, Wednesday and Friday, and evenings by appointment," she said. "If you have other questions, do call. Maybe I can show you *my* collection."

I grinned and pocketed the card. I turned once at the door. She was leaning against the desk, her arms crossed. She gave me the half-inch smile, which I carried with me most of the way back to the car. If she had given me an inch, I'd probably have taken a mile.

18

ᑐᕀᑐᕀᑐᕀᑐᕀᑐ

I STOPPED AT a gas station and used a pay phone while the man filled the tank. I dialed Castle's office, but he was not in. When the receptionist asked if I wanted to leave a message, I said not to bother, that I would catch Joel later. If he mistook the reason I was looking for him, I could expect to find Oscar the Grouch and B.C. camped in my waiting room later, eating their last kill. I got Castle's home number from the directory and dialed.

The answering service was live, which is fine if you want to give only a name and number: but I needed to leave a more detailed message. They are always so eager to get you off the line and get to someone else. Volume is how they make their money. No message, I told her.

It was ten of six. I decided I would try Castle again in awhile, and if the vibes were okay, I could stop by his house on the way back to the city. I went into a posh little cafe with a brass-potted palm and a slate with the evening's menu scrawled on it flanking the door. The dining side was deserted, so I sat at the bar. In Lowell at this hour the house would be packed with workers, joined for a Bud and a shot of V.O., the International Brotherhood of Boilermakers. Mine was a city of barrooms, Catholic churches and funeral parlors. There was an equation in that some-where, but I had never worked it out. Here in Andover the churches tended to tall white spires, and this bar was quiet. If you didn't count the Ms. behind it. She just made the twenty-one age limit and wore teased yellow hair and a micro-skirt in the pattern of a Union Jack that in a few hours would have all the troops saluting.

"You gonna eat?" she asked me. Her accent was about as British as a cheeseburger. "Our special tonight we got jumbo shrimp."

"Nothing like a little oxymoron to start the evening," I said.

She shoved a menu my way. "Just the special and what's on there."

I ordered a Mill City ale and a turkey breast sandwich, which arrived as thick as my fist, and I sat there like one of the idle rich, gnawing at the sandwich and at one little question: was the person who had sold Castle the jade Suoheang Khoy?

At six-thirty I tried Castle at home again but hung up when the service answered. It was not until I was heading home and saw the sign for the Sheraton coming up on my right that I decided to give him the pleasure of an unexpected visit. I slowed and turned into the hidden country lane.

The meadow had a churchyard peacefulness in the shafts of dusty sunlight angling through the pine woods beyond it. The house was more striking than it had been at night, more costly. Walls of glass and redwood came together at architect's angles, and the wide fieldstone chimney jutted above the shake roof grandly. Lawn sprinklers made rainbows on grass the cool green color of numbers on a stock monitor. Castle's blue Rolls sat before the garage at the head of the long driveway. There was no sign of the Town Car or the hired help, which didn't sadden me. I used the doorbell and, when nobody appeared, the brass knocker.

I heard a sound like a door banging shut inside the house, maybe in the back. I waited. Knocked again.

It's the Lifestyles of Poor and Obscure Syndrome. Most people are curious about what goes on behind the high walls and the smoked glass of limousines. Who's doing what to whom? Most people are content to get the dirt on TV or in the tabloids. Most people don't earn their living by their curiosity.

I walked up the driveway past beds of flowers which had the luxuriant offhandedness of an English garden, but I knew as much care had gone into them as into the choice of furnishings inside. I peered at the Rolls. On the driver's door there was some message, presumably Castle's initials, displayed in tiny nautical flags. Inside one of the garage bays was another car, wrapped in a body bag, a Jag maybe, or one of those low-slung Italian jobs that get about two girls to a gallon. There seemed to be a lot of expensive horsepower sitting around unused.

Behind the house, through the seams in a stockade fence, I glimpsed the pool that Castle had crawled out of last night to greet me. A Styrofoam float chair with an empty Corona beer bottle propped in the armrest drifted in the middle. I would find Castle asleep on a chaise longue, Iacocca's latest thriller tented open on his chest. Maybe Lauren would be there too, sweet with oil, trim in a new swimsuit. With a twinge I edged closer and peered through the closed gate. No one was by the pool.

The gate had a security latch which could be opened only from the inside. I poked a ballpoint pen through and lifted it. As I went through, the gate started to swing shut on its springs and would have made a crash if I had not caught it and eased it shut. I thought about the sound I had heard.

There were half a dozen chaises on the Italian-tile apron around the pool, and a big acrylic-topped table with a folded umbrella. In an open cabana in a corner was an Exercycle and a stainless steel barbell set. The water in the pool lay as flat and blue as heaven's eye. The chair floating in it was a mote. I listened to a silence deeper than I'd heard in a long while. A jay called out once from the woods and flitted to a higher branch.

The glass slider on the doorway leading into the house was open an inch. For a full minute I contemplated that fact.

Probably I should have let it be. I edged the slider open six inches. Probably I ought to have closed it. I waited, listening, then opened the door wider. Probably I should have been moving out of there with the vigor of an autumn duck on a late start south. I stepped into the house.

The room I found myself in was the den I had seen the night before, with its recycled drive-in theater screen and fieldstone hearth. Except for the faint sigh of the central AC, the silence was as thick as the carpets. I still did not know what I was doing there or what I was looking for; I only hoped I would when I found it.

Adjoining the den was a formal dining room. Move the table aside and the Celtics could go half-court in it—or the beautiful people dance the night away. The fireplace in the den was backed by an even larger model in here. Above the mantel was a portrait of Himself. It was the "our founder" pose, Castle standing in a dark suit and rich red tie behind a massive leather chair, like a lord of the realm. Citizen Cleen. As I gazed at the swirl of oils, the portrait became like the optical illusion of the transparent cube—the one where, as you stare at it, it keeps flipping back and forth. There was Mr. Joel Castle, whom Lauren and the woman at the antique gallery obviously knew—and then I'd be seeing Joey Costello grinning shrewdly out at me, and I could swear the portrait was Day-Glo colors on black velvet.

I looked away, out the dining room door into the front entry with the big windows, knowing the Lincoln was coming up the drive. But the road lay empty in the declining angle of sunlight. The sprinklers had shut themselves off and the rainbows were gone. No pots of gold anywhere.

I opened a third door off the foyer. Shadowed as the room was by drawn vertical blinds, I nevertheless saw in there the leather chair from the portrait, with its back to me, a plush ox-blood brown. Beyond was a large desk. I saw the shell of a computer monitor and oak file cabinets. I had an idea Castle Cleen was run from corporate suites in one of the office parks on the outskirts of the city, but this would be the private home office which Joel Castle would need. He was a man who would want ready access to his fiefdom any time the spirit moved him, the way Uncle Scrooge liked to go into the counting house and paddle around in his cash. I had taken a few paces forward before the back of my neck prickled in that primitive reaction that we haven't lost.

Sitting in the chair, one hand in his lap, the other hanging off the padded arm, was Castle.

I gobbled breath and spread my feet, getting balance. It did not matter how many times you had been there, you were always a virgin.

133

His head was slumped forward a little. His face had a lumpy pallor, spotted slightly, like the bark of winter birch trees. I probed his throat for a pulse that I knew would not be there. My fingers came back sticky.

The bullet had gone in at close range, a single shot, I judged, behind the left ear. I looked around for the weapon that had fired it, but it wasn't there. Nor were any brochures from the Hemlock Society.

The round had exited through the Adam's apple, just above where a gold pin cinched Castle's shirt collar around the knot of a silk tie that had been some color other than maroon. Blood had run down the front of his blue shirt, and I saw where a congealed drop of it hung from his French cuff like a ruby pendant. Despite the impact of the gunshot, the eyes were open, though dull with that fused-out murk that eyes have when the life has gone from them. Although I knew it was illusion created by the dimness of the room, even that burnished brass hair seemed to have faded.

I drew another breath and felt a pang of regret. Who did this to you, Joey? Why did you let them?

The room had been searched. Here and there a book had been pulled off a shelf, a file drawer and a few desk drawers weren't quite closed. The Daniel Mink watch was gone. Pens and pencils had been poured like pick-up sticks out of a vase on the blotter. Under them lay several spreadsheets containing lists of numbers. I didn't have to guess that the numbers were dollar amounts: long skinny columns, like rope ladders down the sides of a foundering ship. But the life rafts at the ends had not been enough. No amount of dough ever is in the end, when the bottom line for every one of us comes out zero.

Somehow I didn't think the figures had much to do

with Castle's early retirement. The room had been tossed by somebody looking for a more tangible asset than paper, and I had an idea of what.

A new thought pressed me. Had the sound I had heard earlier been made by the killer exiting through the pool gate?

There were two telephones on a corner of the desk: a quaint black model with a rotary dial, and a pearl-gray unit with the handset on the side and more buttons than a sailor's pants. There were settings already coded for the Andover police and fire department I saw, but I used my handkerchief on the receiver of the black phone and dialed the number for the Lowell police. I told the woman who answered who I was and who I wanted. Ed St. Onge came on with a snarl. I told him why I was calling. There was an oasis of silence about ten seconds wide, then: "What brought you there? Social call on a friend?"

"It'll take too long to explain. Just tip the locals, will you? Get them out here."

"Trying to save a dime?" he said tartly.

"Maybe a lot more than that." As I put the phone to bed, my eye fell on a paperweight that looked like a chunk of petrified wood. Actually it was what was underneath that grabbed me. A newspaper clipping. Picking it up I saw it was a blab column from the Lawrence *Eagle-Tribune*.

> **Joel Castle** has shown his exquisite taste once again. The Andover entrepreneur recently purchased a collection of stunning antique jade, including a large Buddha, masks, flowers, and a ring. Speaking of which, Castle hinted he might be giving a ring to a "special friend" when he makes an announcement at his annual open

house later this month. Do we get three guesses, Joel? Are the rest of us jaded ladies going to be *green* with envy?

I did not need even one guess. A gust of fear blew cold across my heart.

19

⊙⊙⊙⊙⊙⊙⊙⊙

Leaving Castle to face his imminent guests alone, I took 93 north to 495 south, keeping the needle at seventy, but not thinking about numbers, thinking that I ought to have called St. Onge right back and had him send a car ahead, that I should have worried more about the fingerprints I'd probably left. But that was just mind-noise now. I didn't know if the killer had seen the clipping or not, but I had to figure that Lauren was the special friend and maybe everyone else knew too.

I hooked onto the Connector and got off at Industrial Avenue. The Wang towers were lit up in the twilight, but traffic was sparse. I was easy pickings for a speed trap, which would mean delay and a fine and a penalty on my record for the next three years—which was about a year longer than you'd pull for homicide these days—but I risked it. In the last stretch I got behind an old party who was moving almost as slow as a cabbie with a fare. I honked and got by him and soon made my turn on squealing tires.

The neighborhood was quiet. The ex-neighbor's lawn gave off a sweet, fresh-cut smell. The other ex-neighbor would be reading the kids Dr. Seuss stories now. Lauren's Honda was in the driveway, and as I started up the walk I had all I could do to keep from sprinting. The mail was still in the box, no lights on inside, no welcoming sounds of TV, or ice in the martini pitcher.

Beyond the aluminum screen the inside door was ajar. I thought of the .38 I kept locked in the bottom drawer of my office file cabinet, as useful now as a ceramic watchdog. I eased the door open but did not go in yet.

"Lauren," I called and felt *"I'm home"* rise in my mind like a ghost. But I was not home. Not anymore.

No reply.

My right hand moved by rote to the light switches, one each for outside, the hallway, living room, coat closet. I hit the middle two and went in fast.

The living room looked like the aftermath of rowdy houseguests.

Adrenaline is the most potent upper there is: zero to sixty in no time. I did not brake to look at anything in particular, just moved through the dining room, scanning. More drawers and the china closet stood open. My heart was thudding as I approached the kitchen. I reached for the wall switch and something whacked the side of my head like the end of a two-by-four.

Fireworks. The blow staggered me. I tried to brace on the kitchen table, but it was not there.

I hit the floor on rubber knees, struggling to stay conscious. From the fogs of Queer Street I made out the smallish man-form as it started past. I grabbed a leg. I was vaguely aware of an Asian face in watery soft focus. The leg I was holding braced, then the other foot swung up fast and kicked at my head. I hunched away, taking the blow on the shoulder, falling backwards with the impact. The attacker bolted for the back door. When I finally got onto the porch and gazed into the thickening dark, nothing was shaking but me.

In the house I put on lights, all of them. Then, dreading it, I went up the stairs to the bedrooms, afraid of what I would find.

The master bedroom had been ransacked, bureau and vanity drawers out, jewelry box upended in a pirates' booty of costume trinkets on the bed. Lampshades sat askew, like the shadows they cast. Lauren was not in any of the rooms. I used the hall phone and called the Lowell police for the second time in an hour.

In the downstairs bathroom I turned on the sink taps, letting the sound of running water soothe me. I washed my face, which was starting to bruise over my right cheek. When I shut off the taps, I heard something else. You learn the sounds a house makes: the appliances, a loose sash, where the floor squeaks when someone steps on it. The unfamiliar ones alert you.

Hurriedly I looked around for a weapon. They are everywhere when you need them. I removed a potted plant from the vitreous china top of the tank behind the toilet. Gripping the heavy lid with both hands, I eased it off and slipped into the hallway. Someone else was in the house, carefully moving my way. I raised the lid, set to break a skull. Lauren stepped through the doorway.

She yelped and I hissed my breath out. I lowered the lid. "You're safe," I said.

"I *better* be. What are you doing here?" She was in her exercise clothes, her face flushed from walking.

"Someone got in."

"It looks like you did! I want to know *why*."

"In the living room—sit down a minute."

"This place is a wreck! What are you after? What's going on?"

I had long ago learned that with bad news there is no good time, nor any useful indirection; the best you could

139

do was the straight truth. "Lauren," I said, as gently as I knew how, "Joel Castle is dead."

That did it. She backed into the front room and dropped onto the couch, her face drained to a pallor. I told her.

20

❧❧❧❧❧❧❧❧

LAUREN REGARDED ME as if I were one long bad news report. The look of suspicion had given way to tears that gleamed in her eyes but did not fall. We sat on the living room couch, straining the silence to its limit. Finally, to be doing something, I said I would make tea.

It had come back to me that the person who had tried to take my head off had been wearing latex gloves, so fingerprints were doubtful. Still, I touched as little as I had to. Moving about, I noted changes—new dishware, furniture rearranged. But it was not all new; the ceramic-handled copper kettle sat on the stove, a wedding gift, a ghost. I half-filled it and set it on a burner. Back in the living room I did not sit again. Lauren had a cigarette burning, which she smoked halfway down in edgy little dabs before crushing it out in a clamshell ashtray.

"The police will be here any minute," I said. "They won't bother you tonight if you don't want, but they'll need to look around. I asked St. Onge not to make it a circus."

Lauren nodded. She seemed collected now, though it was probably numbness.

"Is there any way this makes sense?" I pried gently.

141

"No."

"Had Joel gotten any threats?"

Same answer.

"Was he involved with anything or anyone that might make enemies?"

She closed her eyes a moment and sighed with fraying patience. "No, Alex."

I took out the *Eagle-Trib* column I had swiped from Castle's desk. "What about this?"

Her eyes flicked over it with only a remote flare of interest. "I knew about that. I told Joel the jade ring was part of the collection and ought to be kept with the rest."

"You never got any jade?"

"I got a ruby." She put her hand out and looked at it as if the ring and the finger it was on belonged to someone else.

"Did you ever see his jade collection?"

"I thought you said there wasn't going to be any bother tonight."

I wandered over to the picture window and opened the drapes partway and peered out. No squad car yet. Behind me, from the couch, Lauren sighed. "Yes, I've seen the jade."

I turned.

"He kept the collection at home, for now. You were probably wondering that," she said. "He hoped to acquire one last piece to complete a group. Some kind of dragon."

"Who had that?"

"I don't know."

"Was it the same person who sold him the jade he had?"

"I couldn't say."

"Do you know who the original seller was?"

142

"Look, Joel handled business affairs by himself. It's the way he was. He took responsibility for things, Alex."

The ghost in the kitchen began to whistle.

My nerves wanted chamomile tea, something to soothe them, to cut the adrenaline and put me out of the fray; but I knew the evening was not over yet. I brewed the high-test in two cups with *Far Side* cartoons on them and brought them back to the living room. The police made their well-oiled arrival a minute later: a gray sedan and a squad car, St. Onge and a pair of uniforms. As the patrolmen checked the yard and the forced front door, St. Onge sat with us. Declining tea, he lit a cigarette for Lauren and one for himself. They had always liked each other back when the three of us and Ed's wife, Leona, would get together for dinner and bridge. Lauren said she didn't mind talking, so he took her over some of the same ground we had already covered. When he got to Castle, he asked his questions tactfully, for which I was grateful.

"What about you?" St. Onge said to me. "What can you add?"

I filled him in from the time I had left Castle's to almost braining Lauren with the toilet tank cover. I debated giving him the newspaper clipping, but Lauren had not brought it up, so I didn't. He already had notes on the jade and the fancy wristwatch as possible motive for Castle's death; he didn't need gossip too—or my scattershot guesswork that whoever had killed Castle might have seen the clipping and made the link to Lauren and come after her too, thinking she had jade.

I walked St. Onge through the events there at the house, and we finished up in the kitchen, where I'd been hit.

"Nothing else you remember seeing?" he said.

"Stars mostly. I think he was Asian."

"Based on a foggy glance in a dark room." He shook his head.

When he went out to see how his troops were doing, I sat in the living room with Lauren. She was sunk back deep in the cushions now. In the clamshell on the coffee table, her cigarette grew ash. She was seeing through the furniture and walls.

One of the oil paintings was off-kilter, I noticed. There were a pair of them that went with the abstracts in my office, and they took me back to the little apartment on Varnum Avenue where Lauren and I had lived just after we got married. One day I found half a dozen paintings stacked on the sidewalk with the trash. When you have bare walls and a thin wallet, you take something like that as a sign. In time I learned that our neighbor was an impoverished young painter named Montejo. He would re-use canvas until it was layered so thick with paint it would not take another coat. The rejects—which were most of them then—wound up on our walls by way of the trash pile. The first time I invited him in and showed him, he scowled and said something in Portuguese about someone's mother, but I think he was secretly pleased. He donated some additional paintings before he moved away. I had not heard of him since, but if someone came in one day, recognized the brushstrokes, and said Montejos were selling like hotdogs in SoHo, I was ready. Okay, their outlines and colors were too sharp, the perspective skewed, but I still liked the paintings. They had energy and promise. They took me back to those times on Varnum Avenue. I straightened the one on the wall. Lauren did not seem to notice.

"Want me to stick around?" I said.

She was slow answering, drugged by whatever chemical the body produces to help it cope. "I'm going to call Nancy and Rod and stay with them tonight."

"I can take you over," I said.

"Or maybe I'll go to a hotel."

"You sure you don't want—"

"Positive." She stared at me. "Okay?"

Castle was not the cause of what happened between us. A catalyst maybe, but the change had been in me and in her. It was real, and if I'd known it a day, I'd known it for months. I just had not been able to admit it. Now, a one-word sentence had shown me. Signatures on paper were only a formality. "Okay," I said.

I found St. Onge in the driveway, talking on the sedan's radio. He had folded his jacket and hung it over the open car door. Neighbors were watching through parted curtains, but no one had ventured over. Ed slung the mike.

"Hot town," he said, "summer in the city."

I looked at him.

"There are impressions in the grass in back where someone took off on foot. Probably had wheels down the block. I'll have a cruising patrol keep an eye peeled. We'll canvass the neighbors in the A.M., see if anyone saw something."

"A small white car maybe, white wheel covers?" I shook my head. "The guy who was here had on gloves, which says he was careful. You should still tell Andover to print Castle's place. They'll find mine, but that was afterwards. And someone ought to check the woods beside his house. If that was the pool gate I heard, the killer could have parked at the Sheraton and come and gone through the woods."

"You writing a text on investigative practice?"

"No."

Ed nodded tiredly. "You could've called the locals directly. That's going to raise questions."

It was his way of asking again what I had been doing at Castle's in the first place. I stayed dumb. He said he would talk to a sergeant he knew on the Andover force. We listened to crickets and the garble of the sedan's two-way for a moment, then he took his coat off the door and tossed it onto the front seat. "I'm going to keep a patrolman here awhile."

"Lauren may stay with friends tonight."

He angled his head toward the lighted windows of the living room. "Any chance you two patching things up?"

I noticed for the first time that the drapes were different, brighter. "That's history," I said. "Like a lot of things about this city."

I drove back downtown and cruised by the darkened DSS office, just to assure myself that Ada was long gone. I had forgotten to call her as I had said I would. It was after ten when I got home. Maybe not too late on a Friday night . . .

"Mea culpa," I said when she answered.

"I guess I was just last on a list of things to do," she said in a tone I couldn't read.

"The evening got hectic. I'm sorry."

"Uh-huh."

"You were sleeping?"

"Not anymore. In fact, I'm thinking about going out to meet someone. There's a good jazz group at the Hilton. Interested?"

"I'd be a lousy third person," I said.

"Who said anything about three?"

21

⊘⊙⊙⊘⊙⊙⊘⊙⊙

AT ELEVEN P.M. Ada Chan Stewart got out of a Diamond cab in the circular drive under the Hilton awning and came through the plate glass doors into the lobby like a sweet dream after a jag of nightmares. Until that moment I had been giving myself excuses for why I was not up to this. All at once I didn't want one. She was wearing a deep iridescent green dress that went to mid-calf and swished and clung and showed off the lower part of her legs, which flexed in the black medium-heels she wore. She held a tiny black-beaded purse and had on a wide-brimmed hat of black straw, tipped at an angle, and she smiled from under it when she saw me. I had showered and put on my pale gray summerweight suit.

The lounge was not too busy as we went in, and I loved the way she put her hand on my arm as though it belonged there. Some women can do that without it becoming a big deal. We got a booth separated from the bar by a low partition with ferns growing in a trough on top. A waitress lit the candle, and we ordered a pair of gin and tonics. The group was into a set, four musicians, racially divided, and a Latino female vocalist who was doing a sultry "Teach Me Tonight."

We got caught up. She reported her day in the trenches

with such energy I got the feeling we were winning. I began to fill her in on my day. The smile she had gotten when I told what Ms. Sydney Keyes at the Haskell and MacKay Gallery had said about her turned to seriousness when I got to the next part. I hesitated only on the most recent stretch, involving Lauren, then I told that too. Not to would have left a gap that I did not want to have to scurry around later to backfill and then worry whether I had filled it enough. Ada was a good listener, though maybe it was just the training.

"She's probably in emotional limbo now," Ada said. "God knows I would be. She'll come out of it. She sounds level-headed."

"She's that," I agreed.

"Perhaps this will bring you back together."

I shook my head. "Tonight I saw what I've been avoiding. I just hadn't found the words yet."

I said no more, and Ada knew to let it lie. But there was the fact of Joel Castle's death. I had told her my uneasy suspicions. After a spell she said, "So you really think Joel Castle's death is connected with Bhuntan's?"

"Do you want to talk about this now?" I asked.

"I think we have to."

I had already told her what Samol Lim had revealed about the Khmer Rouge executions. Now I said, "The gunshot pattern is too similar not to consider it. But we'll have to wait to hear what the investigators find. If the two are linked, there's only one point of juncture I can see."

"The jade."

"Stone of heaven."

She thought a moment before saying, "Does that mean you think Suoheang Khoy might be around?" She sounded surprised, and I was too—that she had remembered the name.

"I haven't got that far yet," I said. "And right now, I don't want to." I ordered new drinks.

In a booth across from us, a silver-haired man took out a cigar that looked like it had been manufactured by a large dog and slowly, lovingly got it going. If he paid his wife half the attention he was bestowing on the cigar, he had a happy marriage—though why did I doubt the babe he was with was his wife? And why was I thinking about wives anyway?

Ada said, "It's amazing what you've accomplished. But it's a little frightening. I don't like you getting hurt."

"Let's form a club," I said.

"I mean it."

"Maybe I should get some tattoos for protection. Lim showed me his. Do the women get them too?"

"No."

"Give them a generation to assimilate. Tattoos are one of the little extras that slipped across the gender lines during the women's revolt, along with ulcers and neckties. One that got turned back at the border was cigars. I've yet to meet a woman who smoked them, or wanted to."

Her mind was not on the patter, so I quit. "What say we dance before the sprinklers go off."

We slipped her purse into my coat pocket and waded to the parquet, where half a dozen other couples were drifting easily to a mellow reading of "For Sentimental Reasons."

The vocalist was a reed-thin, intense woman, the tenor player a large, sloe-eyed black man whose shaved head gleamed like an ebony newel post. As unalike as they seemed, they had a nice magic working. Despite her starved look, she got a lot of South American lushness into her phrasing. His solos were spare and cool until they went hot enough to water drinks in the room. The piano,

149

drums and bass backgrounded nicely, stepping out to blow solo, then melting back into the lineup.

In her heels, Ada came to where her head nuzzled the hinge of my fresh-shaven jaw. I liked it that she was not skinny. There was flesh on her and she moved fluidly in my arms. She made me feel like Patrick Swayze. Our heat released an incense of jasmine. We stayed on the floor. When the band broke, we got another round of drinks and took them onto the outdoor patio overlooking the canal. Ada's cheeks were flushed from the dancing. She drew the conversation back to before.

"So Bhuntan's killing may tie in with others," she said.

"May. The rest adds up to less than zero so far. Except for the bill. If I were you I'd keep the escape clause open."

"I'm determined."

"You had me fooled. Anyway, this isn't client and gumshoe tonight, I hope. I punched out when the last of the trail dust swirled down the shower drain."

Her eyes had not left mine. In the gleam of the tiny white lights strung through the ficus trees in their big terra cotta urns on the patio, they were silky and bright and wise. "Friends?" she offered tentatively.

"I could use one."

We drank to it, then Ada took her purse and excused herself to go find the powder room. I leaned on the railing and looked down at the starlight in the deep black water.

In the 1790s the Pawtucket Canal had run right by this spot. A mile and a half long and dug by hand to bypass the Merrimack's thirty-foot falls, the canal helped water the roots of what blossomed thirty years later as industrial America. After a visit to England, Francis Cabot Lowell brought back a head full of ideas for factory machines. Other canals followed, tapping the supply of immigrant labor and the energy of the river to run textile mills. Dubbed the Venice of America, Lowell boomed through the century, drawing each new wave of workers to tend the machines. The labor movement got its impetus here too, complete with strikes and headbusting, scabs and prototype Jimmy Hoffas. By the 1930s, however, with depression and the competition of cheap sweat in the South, the city bottomed out and stayed down for four decades. Hard times toughen people who survive them, and the rawboned resilience never went away. Now Renaissance was a term the Chamber of Commerce and the media used. But rebirth did not reach everywhere. I found myself thinking about the distance between Bhuntan Tran and Joel Castle. And yet . . . had something linked them in death? I could not shake the question, nor could I answer it.

So I let it be. Here, off the streets, with starlight winking in the canal, I imagined all of that as far away. Ada's sweet scent was still in my nostrils. I shut my eyes and savored it.

"Penny," the lady herself said beside me.

I didn't see any powder on her nose, but she looked good anyway. "Throwing your money away again," I said.

"What are trust funds for? To quote a friend." She smiled wickedly.

We turned back to the rail, like passengers on an ocean liner in a calm, dark sea. It had occurred to me that in all my years in the city, I could not remember a night without sirens. Ambulances, cop cars, fire trucks—always some crisis, someone's life in turmoil. But tonight . . . "Peaceful," I said.

We listened to the stillness, then looked at each other for confirmation.

151

She said, "It's nice."

I put my hand lightly on her arm near the shoulder and bent my head into the fragrant space thus formed.

The kiss had all those qualities of the first one that are never there again in the same parts: mystery and softness, gentle fear, wonder, electricity, lust.

"Alex," she murmured after our lips had moved back to the distance of a breath.

If only we had let that be enough for the moment, if we had gone back to the music that the band had started to make again. We were too hungry.

"Alex," she said again, but differently, "I don't ask much . . . but today, I finally let myself remember where I'd heard your name before. I got one of the secretaries in the office to fill in the rest."

Had I drawn back another step? "You could have just asked me. I figured you already knew."

"I was thinking about you, and I wanted to know at that moment right then. Were you dismissed from the police for taking a bribe?"

"Did you stay for the whole show?"

"I know only that. And that the charges were never proven in a court hearing. But I don't care about it. You can tell me, that's what I'll go on. You didn't really take money, did you?"

I considered making it easy—the night was so full of stars and promise, the sweet siren of jazz and gin. Maybe that's why I couldn't. There was a point in any linkup between people when either you told the truth or you lied, and that set the rules. Everything else followed the path you chose that moment.

I said, "I took it."

Her eyes got a tunneled look and she nodded. "Oh."

I started to say more, but she looked away so quickly that any words were lost.

"It's getting late," she whispered. She took her purse off the railing. "I'll have the doorman get me a cab."

I watched her, wanting to say something to lessen the blow, to apologize in some way, but there had been enough of that tonight already. I trailed her back inside and then out, looking on mutely as she got into the cab and it looped off, leaving me rooted on the sidewalk like a lone pine tree the bulldozer has spared. Inside the hotel lounge the band did a moody intro to " 'Round Midnight." The piano sounded a little off, although it was probably me. Their timing was right on though, as confirmed by my watch. As I walked to the parking garage, I heard the distant goosehonk of fire engines. I had spoken too soon about the silence. Trouble did not quit just because you wanted it to.

22

❧❧❧❧❧❧❧

I SPENT SATURDAY morning with plainclothes cops in Andover, a fresh-faced pair, one short with a pale brown crew cut and sunglasses hanging around his neck on a cord, the other sturdy, dark, moustached. They would have looked good on prime time. But then crime in their town tended to stock swindles and art theft and Potter and Kit over at the Phillips going on a rampage and toilet-papering the maple trees on the town common. We walked through the crime scene at Joel Castle's, then sat in their car in the Sheraton parking lot. They had already checked with the motel staff about suspicious activity the night before. They had asked about a small white car. Nothing. Now they wanted to know all about my involvement with Mr. Castle. I guess when people make your salary worthwhile, you call them Mr. They called me Rasmussen.

I told them what I could. The problem came when I reached the part I could not. They looked at each other in the front seat, maybe cuing a rehearsed role play, then looked back to where I sat in the rear of the unmarked Crown Vic. I was grateful for the car. The patrol cars there are white with red and blue stripes; I would have felt silly sitting in one of them. The cop with the moustache said, "The woman from the Haskell and MacKay Gallery called us soon as she heard the eleven o'clock news report that Mr. Castle had been murdered. She gave your name—the same name as the person who called Lowell police to say he'd found the victim."

We had been all over that. With the sun on the roof, the car was getting hot inside. We were all being polite about not sweating, but I was getting close.

"Let me understand this," said Crewcut, resting his arm on the steering wheel and twisting to eye me. "You went back there last night to ask Mr. Castle some questions about his jade collection?"

"Right." I had said nothing about Lauren's relationship with Castle; why give people motive where none exists?

"Do you always walk into people's houses uninvited?"

"I'm trying to quit."

Moustache gave me a warning look. I had already told them about the sound I had heard. I was getting bored hearing myself. "What was your interest in the jade?" he asked.

"Professional, like I said."

"A case you're working on."

"Right."

"For whom?"

I smiled into his eyes. They were that bright, watery blue-green shade that some people like in their toilet bowls.

"Don't pull client privilege with us," Crewcut said. "We've got ways around it."

I doubted it. When you've had Francis X. Droney searing your shirt collar with his breath, you don't sweat a crew-cut Michael J. Fox.

155

"Statistically," he went on, "the odds point to the one who reports a killing as the killer."

Cops are your friends until they're not. Treat me nice, I roll over and let you scratch my belly; but I can go the other way and snarl and bite your foot if you swing it. "That stat only works if the two were related or romantically involved," I said. "We weren't. Check the M.E.'s report for time of death then get back to me. The woman at Haskell and MacKay was probably still propositioning me at that point. As for the rest of it, you don't need to know my client's name. There's no connection, so why clutter your report with irrelevant details? You both took freshman comp."

They swapped another look, as if trying to decide what they could hold me on. But they knew the score; it would mean trying to justify a bust on a phony obstruction charge, and with the judges we had in this state, that would be tough. Hell, second-degree murder got you about six months. It did not hurt either that St. Onge had vouched for me. As we sat there scowling, a pair of deeply tanned young women in French-cut swimsuits and fluorescent Vuarnet T-shirts came out of the hotel with canvas beach bags. Crewcut slipped his sunglasses on, and the three of us watched, united for a moment in something. The women hopped into a graphite gray BMW and got a little bun warming on the hot upholstery. In a few seconds the AC was blowing cool across them like the breath of youth.

"So you don't even think Mr. Castle brought this on himself?" Crewcut said in a lighter tone, turning back and letting his shades hang again.

"If so, it was by advertising. Some people figure goodies are worthless unless other people know you've got them."

I sent another look toward the girls in the BMW, but they had the tinted windows up now.

"But as for being into anything dirty . . . ?" the cop said.

"Only other folks' laundry, as far as I can tell."

I found it odd to be defending Joel Castle, but in spite of all of his smooth, polished parts that fit so well in this town, there had remained one small rough edge that was pure Lowell.

"So why did he employ those two goons?" Moustache asked.

"Personal assistant and chauffeur," I corrected.

"They're both Concord grads, you know."

I knew he didn't mean the prep school. "I wondered about that too, but it makes a kind of sense. Some people keep big ugly dogs to scare away folks they don't want around. From what I saw, everyone got fed and patted in the deal. You suspect them?"

"No," said Crewcut. "They were at the airport in Boston last night, waiting to pick up someone who never showed. A state trooper confirms it. He ticketed the Lincoln for being in a taxi zone."

I did not pursue that, but I stored it away. There were a few more questions, then Crewcut started the Ford. "In case we all need to do this again," he said, "you aren't planning to go away anytime soon, are you?"

I gave them my most law-abiding grin. "Not unless you're buying the ticket."

I pulled into a McDonald's on 133. Inside I found a phone and punched in the code to get my messages. Make that message. St. Onge had called to say he was having a late lunch at the Athenian Corner downtown if I cared to join him. Somehow it did not sound like a suggestion.

I found him sitting by the window working on a piece of moussaka the size of a paving stone and sipping retsina. I could not see if there was a flare on his pants cuffs, but the sports jacket had lapels that a sunflower boutonniere wouldn't have looked out of scale on. I ordered salad. The place was between lunch and dinner hours, and we had the corner to ourselves, surrounded by leggy philodendrons and the clutter of decorative decanters and gimcrack souvenirs that Greek restaurateurs think constitute interior design.

"This a date?" I asked.

He swished the retsina like mouthwash and swallowed. I could see the whiskers on his cheeks as they puffed with a suppressed belch. He pushed his plate away and lit a cigarette. "I felt like hell being over there last night," he said. "Lauren's one good woman."

"Thanks for clueing me."

"Not for you," he said irritably. His eyes were as dark as Calamata olives. "I was sad for all of us. You, me, the wives. We used to have good times."

"Our hearts were young and gay," I said.

I nibbled salad. He smoked in silence. Finally he said, "Negative on any car last night. No one in that neighborhood saw nothing. I know, it's a double negative."

"I wasn't going to say a word."

"It's the way I feel. Christ, instead of birdbaths and trolls, people ought to just put three fucking monkeys on their lawns these days. Nobody wants involvement for shit."

"Do you kiss your wife and kids with that mouth?"

"It's about *all* I do with them lately."

He finished the wine and got the waitress's eye by raising the empty glass. "You done with that rabbit food?"

158

"You want to finish it?"

He scowled and ground out his cigarette in the salad and lit another one. I recounted for him my session with the TV cops from Andover.

"Castle is *their* problem. Tran is still mine."

"And?"

"Life seems to have an odor lately," he said metaphysically. "I clued Droney on last night's events. He's not interested in a big maze of might-bes. He likes the shake-and-bake ones. Homicide Helper. Man hits wife with an ax and eats a bullet. Druggies smoke each other in a deal gone sour. The ones that give neat headlines. These complicated jobs only make everyone look bad."

The waitress brought him another glass of wine, which he lifted into a shaft of smoky sunlight so that it sparkled. "I'd like to hang around the rest of the afternoon and get bingoed. Interested?"

"You'd only ramble and reminisce and recount old tales in a voice grown faintly wistful," I said, "and wake up later with a taste in your mouth like you'd been licking gun barrels. What you need is a new set of lenses. Go see an optimist."

He shook his head wonderingly. "Look at me. Saturday afternoon and I'm working. I've got a raft of paper that high on my desk. My family's turning into a single-parent home. And Leona—she's great about it, you know her—but it's like . . . there's no balance anymore."

"You're obviously not looking for sage counsel by telling me."

He tapped ashes into the salad and sucked smoke. "Bitching helps."

"Well, here's old news. You're right. The pile doesn't get any shorter. You keep taking it off the bottom, they

159

keep putting it on the top, and one day someone else is in your chair deciding what to pitch. So lock up for the weekend and go home and take everyone out for miniature golf and the drive-in theater. Go to Crane's Beach tomorrow and get a lease on a sunburn and eat hot dogs with your sand. Life's short all over."

His mouth twisted under the steel gray threads of his moustache. "Old news, but it's good to hear. Maybe I will." In a lowered voice he said, "So what the hell, here's something on the Castle burn. Along with the fancy watch, a wall safe in his bedroom was jimmied and cleaned out."

"I'll bet I know what was inside. Any prints?"

"Not up there. Downstairs there were more prints than on a diner spoon. The locals even managed to lift some, including yours and those gazoonies Castle had working for him. But there was one set hasn't been ID'd yet. It's got priority. Ditto with ballistics. Results should come in tomorrow."

"When you're at the beach," I said.

"Interesting?" he said.

I shrugged. "Maybe I'll catch it all in the newspaper."

He narrowed his eyes.

"I don't have a client anymore," I said. "I think I've been axed."

23

ADA STEWART WAS in my waiting room when I got back at three P.M. She set aside a copy of *Time* so old it still thought Michael and Janet Jackson were two different people, and we looked at each other with mute discomfort. I hung my jacket on the coat tree and put a couple of important turns in each shirt sleeve. I would have liked about ten arms.

"You caught up on ancient history?" I asked. "Or were you casing the paintings? They're original ash can school."

"I want to hear it, Alex, all of it. But no jokes. I didn't sleep well last night."

She hadn't. Her eyes were dark-circled and her lips were drawn, not the lips I had tasted so briefly last night.

I unlocked the office and followed her inside. She took the chair she had sat in five days ago. With another key I unlocked the file cabinet and hauled open the bottom drawer. The licensed Smith & Wesson K38 Masterpiece was in there in the same snap-top holster I had kept it in for years. There was also a fifth of George Dickel. I let them both lie. I reached for the big envelope nestled flat behind the gun and the bourbon.

There was an envelope just like it in a security drawer at

the Enterprise Bank and Trust downtown. I set this one on the desk and sat in my chair and unwound the little string that sealed the flap. I drew out three file folders, one of which I slid across to her. It held clippings from the local and Boston newspapers.

While she read, I paged through a second folder, the fattest of the three. It contained a transcript of the probable cause hearing, plus my own notes. The third folder, the thinnest, had the department's official action. Francis X. Droney's name and signature appeared quite often.

The office was as quiet as a library carrel where we might have been cramming for a tough final. For once I was grateful for the telephone's silence. Afternoon sunlight crept across the walls on little mice feet. From the street the sounds of Saturday afternoon floated up through the open windows. A car with its radio turned up loud paused at the traffic light, and I heard the ball game from Fenway, where Greenwell and Vaughn had a cottage industry going, turning fastballs into souvenirs. At last Ada closed the file and set it on the desk.

"So taking the bribe was intentional?" she said.

"It was supposed to have been a sting. I worked with a state cop named Rydell and a supervisor—who's gone now, retired to Phoenix—just the three of us. We didn't want any leaks. The councilman was shaking down developers who hoped to build in the area. With the city economy going through the roof at the time, people wanted in and were willing to buy a ticket. We let the councilman know we knew."

"Though you didn't really have evidence, apparently," Ada said.

"Not enough. We met with the guy, who indicated he'd make it worth our while to help him out. Not in any words you could take to court, of course. We worked it so the

162

statie, Rydell, was wearing a voice-actuated recorder and battery pack taped to his body. I was to take the money. It was set for midnight in the courtyard behind the old Boote Mills complex. Only something went wrong. When we got there, nobody showed."

"They were late?" Ada said.

I shook my head. "With that kind of thing, you're either on the dot, or not at all. We should've scrammed. But we didn't. Rydell took cover, and I walked down into the courtyard. As I stood there, I heard something. Someone walking on broken glass. It was too late to get Rydell there. A bearded guy appeared, said the agreed upon password, and handed me the satchel. I took it. As I did, someone started shooting from the mill. I drew my weapon and returned fire. Rydell did too. He was hit in the face. By the time reinforcements came, the guy with the beard had vanished. The gunman was dead."

"Oh, God."

"He turned out to be hired help from the Bronx. Rydell made it, but he ended up with about a year of memory gone."

"He has no recollection of that evening at all?"

"What evening? A big nothing. Just a lot of hassles, a busted marriage, therapy afterwards. He took his state pension and got a job selling vinyl siding by telephone. Meanwhile, he keeps hoping that some day he'll get back what he lost.

"His wife?"

"His memory. But I'm not holding my breath. The weird thing—when we got him in, there was no wire on him."

Ada frowned. "You mean the councilman's people took it when he was shot?"

"I want to believe that."

"What's the alternative? If he never . . ." She answered her own question. "Oh, no."

"I don't have the answers yet. I did have the bills on me though. Which was enough for most people."

She said nothing for several moments, then: "Can I ask the name of the councilman?"

"Cavanaugh."

"Oh, boy. Mr. Incumbent."

"Still kissing hands and shaking babies. The link with extortion, conspiracy, and intent to murder a police officer never materialized."

Ada was slowly shaking her head. "And he's been one of social service's biggest boosters this year."

I smiled. "At least some good's come out of it. He wants to keep super clean now because he knows somebody knows."

She set the folder on the desk. "So this stays open?"

"For me it does. Until I can close the drawer on it for good." Or until they closed one on me, I thought. Though the way things were going, there wouldn't be anyone for it to matter to either way. "I've got to figure whoever set me up is still around, and so am I. I'm a finger in his eye, a stone in his shoe. A small one, but I'm there. I'll find him. Them."

"And you'll put Cavanaugh away?" Ada said.

"Only when I've got all the ducks straight. A guy as crooked as he is will have law school profs lining up to defend his constitutional rights."

Ada tipped her head to one side. "Couldn't you just go shoot him?"

She ventured her first smile of the afternoon, a little wry at the edges, and brief, but it was a great start. I put the folder back in the file drawer and lifted George Dickel by his neck. Ada nodded. I quarter-filled two glasses and added some spring water and put the bottle back and locked the drawer.

"To honor," she said as we touched glasses.

"Doesn't sound like much fun."

We drank.

"You doing anything tonight?" I asked.

She raised her eyebrows tentatively. "Quiet evening at home with a friend?"

"That sounds a lot funner."

24

ꙮꙮꙮꙮ

So what do I know? With four million in the bank, there are not many houses ruled out on account of price. None in Lowell. But the scion of the Stewart fortune had chosen a plain, two-story wood-frame on Christian Hill with a pair of big sugar maples soughing in the small front yard.

On the way we stopped to do a little domestic number, whisking a shopping basket through busy supermarket aisles where the only language you did not hear spoken was English. We picked up the makings for dinner, and I dropped a twenty on a Pouilly-Fuissé and let it age another fifteen minutes. With Michael Franks on her CD player and the sun sliding down behind the distant New Hampshire hills, Ada did a stir-fry with vegetables, cashews, and tofu. Afterwards she came across the deck and set herself comfortably on my lap, and we sat for a long spell watching the sky dim. Someone a few houses away set off skyrockets, and we laughed. When dusk was full and the bottle empty, she rose and took my hand and we went inside to her bedroom.

We undressed each other, shedding clothes the way you do, with the eagerness of kids opening presents on Christmas. When the gift wrap was gone, she kissed me. Before I could fairly kiss her back, she skipped free and went into the adjoining bathroom. I fumbled my way downstairs. I did not know how to work the CD player, so I slipped an old Oscar Peterson LP out of its jacket and sleeve. I know how to work records. As Peterson's piano began stringing through the moonlit house, I returned and saw Ada standing looking out the bedroom window, saw the curve of her bottom and thought I would like to see the bikini that had made those tan lines.

She came to me with a velvety purr of pleasure, her mouth minty with toothpaste, and we kissed in a fever and when the time was right we lay on the cool sheets and I felt a small shiver prickle her with gooseflesh that caught me too, and we moved together slowly, then quickly. Afterwards I felt her eyelashes on my face, and I tipped my head back and looked at her. She smiled for me.

Moonlight gleamed on the maple leaves beyond the window of the bedroom where Ada lay on her side, propped on an elbow, watching me. I watched her right back. The sheet was tented over my raised knee like a cool mountain in the dark. The house had been silent a long time. Her fingers found the little puckered scar on my shoulder and asked the question in the way they touched it.

"Old mishap," I said.

She shifted position. "From a gunshot, isn't it?"

Her face was a few feet from mine, but except for the gleam of her eyes, I could only just make it out. With a finger I brushed her lips.

"You think I'm someone else," she said after a silence.

"You better not be."

She shifted again, her eyes never leaving mine. "You don't think I'm someone who's technically kidnapped a

167

child and brought it here for its own safety and then had the mother attack me with a hot iron the next time I went to her apartment. Or who's had men push me against a wall and press boozy mouths on me so my only defense was to knee them where it always hurts. I've seen people put needles in their arms, and beat up on the ones they're supposed to love."

"You're one tough kid."

She looked away.

"You're right," I said.

"About what?"

"It's a gunshot wound."

"On the job?"

"The old job."

She sat up, drawing the sheet around her, her face in a shaft of moonlight now as she brought her chin to rest on her knees. "I was thinking tonight . . . Bhuntan's name is clear as far as I'm concerned. That was the thing I wanted when I hired you. I'll request a meeting with the Cambodian Mutual Assistance Association and present what you've found."

"Is that what you want to do? Even though nothing's proved?"

"The police can handle the rest."

"Maybe. I'm not sure they've got the motivation right now."

"It doesn't matter then. I don't want you taking chances. I'll pay you for everything you've done." She was quiet a moment. "Say something."

"Time was," I said, "when that's how lunatics were made."

"What?"

"Sitting in the light of the moon like that."

"I'm serious, Alex."

I sat up too. "It isn't the money anymore," I said.

"You mean you won't stop?"

"There are people who have died, Ada. Maybe I can keep it from happening again. Because I think someone means for it to."

Her bare shoulders clenched with a shudder. "What if you can't?"

"What if I can?"

"You could become a victim yourself."

"With a tough character like you to look out for me?"

She got out of bed and padded across the room to the window. I looked at her in the moonlight, shadows showing the dimples in her lower back and her hips and the smooth swelled curve of her buttocks down into her legs, and I knew one thing. I didn't want to be alone, not there in the night, not in my life. I got up and went across the carpet. She turned and I saw the gleam of wetness on her cheeks and saw her smile bravely. As I reached for her I thought: Grab this, Rasmussen, because you won't find it again, a one-of-a-kind piece like rare jade, with all the handiwork of the master carver.

Hours later something woke me and I saw the moon had set. I laid a hand on the tilt of Ada's back and whispered her name. She made a sleepy sound.

"Do you have a pair of nylons?"

Her muttered words could have been "top drawer bureau," or nothing at all. I checked the big lacquered Chinese bureau whose drawers exhaled the jasmine scent I knew so well. I found a fresh packet of pantyhose and took it quietly into the bathroom where I pulled the door partway closed and put on one of the globed lights flanking the medicine cabinet.

I tore open the nylons. Haynes, the gentleman's preference, size small, sheer. There was no gentleman present, as one glance in the mirror confirmed. I ignored the sleep-bleared presence by opening the cabinet. Inside I found a tiny pair of surgical scissors. There was also a stick of eyeliner. Slowly, carefully I did my eyes, bringing the corners up, elongating and thinning the shape. Then I used the dainty shears to trim the dainty sheers, snipping off half of one leg.

"Is this something we should talk about?"

Ada was leaning sleepily in the doorway. She had on a pale blue silk kimono with a darker brocade dragon guarding each breast and red piping running throat to hem, which came to mid-point on her golden thighs.

"Tell me something," I said. I pulled the cut stocking over my head, working at it in the mirror a moment before I turned. "Could I be a long-lost cousin?"

She gazed and blinked.

The upward tug of nylon over the lined eyes, and the nose-flattening effect, made me Oriental. "Could be," she said. "Strange inspiration."

I yanked the stocking off and pushed back my hair. "I've got a strange muse."

"What does it prove?"

"Only that the man I saw at Lauren's last night didn't have to be Asian." I shrugged, losing my inspiration. "Just an idea I woke up with."

"I woke up with an idea too," she said.

She had not moved. She was still leaning easily in the doorway, arms across her chest, the red-piped hem riding high on one round hip. Victoria's Secret would have paid handsomely for the negative, but I wasn't selling. I dampened a face cloth and swiped it across my eyes. It did wonders for my vision. When I looked again, the kimono was hanging on the doorknob.

I woke to daylight and the whisper of Ada's breath on my jaw like a shared secret. My arm was snugged around her, as asleep as she, but she was curled so warmly into the space I did not move. Sunday morning. I had an image of us lounging around, lazy as a pair of pet store puppies. The sheet had come off her top leg, which curved from the swell of her flank to her delicate golden toes. I started to smile. I could not help myself.

I eased loose and gathered my clothes and moved quietly to the shower door, where I stopped to look back. Ada lay deep in some final dream. I hoped it was about her favorite private eye. Downstairs in the kitchen I found a teapot and some loose black tea and started the water. I used the telephone on the counter.

"What?" St. Onge answered in an annoyed tone.

Why wasn't I surprised to find him in his office? "Wanted to catch you before you left for the beach," I said.

He grunted.

"Any word on the prints at Castle's place?"

"I thought you got canned."

"That was malicious rumor."

Another grunt. "Not yet. Ballistics came through, though. Same gun that was used on Tran."

After a moment's hesitation, I agreed to meet him for coffee. I shut off the kettle. Ada was still sleeping. I looked around for something to leave a note on. There were several envelopes on the counter, utility bills and something from a mortgage company. Through a little cellophane window I saw the name Mrs. Ada Stewart. *Mrs.?* Colonial

171

Gas had her listed that way too. The envelope was open, so I slipped the bill out.

It was an overdue notice to the tune of a hundred bucks, threatening that the gas would be shut off if the bill was not paid immediately. The telephone bill was in Ada's "Miss" incarnation, but it too showed an outstanding balance. The mortgage company statement indicated she had made late payments twice already this year.

Snooperman. Suspicion is my trade. Ada's pocketbook lay on a living room chair, where she'd dropped it last night. There was a checkbook inside in a pebbled gray leatherette folder. The balance, which had been meticulously carried forward in pencil, a detail out of phase with the overdue bills, was $211.76. Two lines above was the entry of the check for three hundred which she had given me.

Ada's voice startled me.

An answering machine on the kitchen counter had kicked on. Ada must have left on the unit down here and put the phones on mute last night; there had been no ring. After the beep a man said: "Darling. Are you there?" Pause. "I guess not. You're up and out early for a Sunday. I hope you won't be tired later. I'm going to the village for lox and bagels, then I'll be at receptions till noon. So, uh, I'll call you when I get a minute. Or you can try me." He left a number. "I'm dying to know what's happening with everything. Ciao for now."

Forget the TV stuff. This work has almost no shoot-outs. The car chases are unwitting, generally the by-product of tailing a Massachusetts driver. The bulk of the time is spent polishing your pants. The callous on my trigger finger is from dialing phones. With a sizable private library of directories from around the Northeast, I know area codes: 212 is Manhattan. Did that make the village Greenwich?

172

But it was the "darling" and the envelopes on the counter that had me wondering. I tried to think of something witty to write for posterity, but what kept coming up had to do with how hard it is to break fortune cookies neatly. I wrote: *"Had to run. Call you later."* I skipped the "ciao mein."

It would have made a cheap telegram.

25

꧁꧂꧁꧂꧁꧂꧁꧂

TEN O'CLOCK MONDAY morning, under a sky as gray as last month's bedsheets, I drove over to Edson Cemetery. I beat the cortege and parked inside along a spiked iron fence, in view of where a backhoe had boxed out Joel Castle's final home. The earth was mounded nearby, covered with a mat of artificial turf. A canopy had been set up, and beneath that stood rows of folding wooden chairs. From the sky came an ominous rumbling. I did not have to wait long before cars with their headlights on began to wind through the gate and along the paved avenues of the dead. No one was going to accuse me of being a big Joel Castle fan, but in the end I had come to accept him. Now I wanted to lay to rest along with him any lingering rumor that I had put him here.

My charcoal wool suit had hung in the closet so long that I had brushed epaulets of dust from the shoulders that morning as I took it off the hanger. I had discovered pinned to the lining a red paper tag bearing the logo of Castle Cleen. Fate has some great gag writers.

No sooner had the mourners emerged from the cars than light rain started to fall, sizzling on the warm pavement. Black umbrellas began to snap open like bat wings. The mortuary service provided loaners for people who had not counted on this one added bleakness. Neither family nor close personal friend, I kept a distance, getting wet. The poet might claim the heavens were weeping for Castle. I say it was just raining.

The pallbearers brought the casket, a brushed bronze affair in the same rich Neapolitan blue as its occupant's Rolls Royce. Wet buds from the maple trees pasted themselves on the metal, providing the only natural touch I could see. The ersatz turf was no more lifelike than the job the mortician would have inflicted on Castle. The ancient Egyptians sent their dead off in well-stocked boats for the after-life journey. I thought about what Syd Keyes at the Haskell and MacKay Gallery had said about jade cicadas.

I estimated the crowd at four or five hundred, including a lot of big money and a scattering of Greater Boston household faces. What did people say? That I'm going to the funeral of my dry cleaner? It didn't sound any worse than saying you were going to send off your private eye. I spotted Bob Whitaker from the *Sun* in his old military poncho, keeping a discreet distance, shooting with a long lens. The editors had known it would be one of the best celebrity turnouts since they had buried Jack Kerouac a few grassy aisles away. The funeral home pros stood to one side under the dripping trees, cupping cigarettes and waiting. A stocky man with shiny dewlaps and a black Chesterfield coat began to speak about his friend in slow, reverential tones over a background of sobs.

I saw Lauren. She was on the opposite side of the grave, seated among a group of old and new friends and members of the family. She looked dignified and pained and beautiful, and it stabbed me to realize she and Castle would have been an attractive couple.

"They should plant him upright," a voice murmured at my ear.

St. Onge stepped up beside me, buttoning his raincoat

175

with slow fingers. Water was beaded in his moustache. "With all that pretty hair sticking up like golden grass," he said. "Give society something for a change. God knows he didn't while he was breathing."

"Be charitable," I admonished.

"Charitable my toe. Castle never was, except when it suited him."

"I guess you didn't idle yesterday away at the beach."

"I spent it working, same as today." His coal-chip eyes measured me. "I'm curious to see who his friends and enemies were."

"Put me down as none of the above," I said.

"Look at this crew. You know what their net worth must be?"

I shrugged. "Death's the great equalizer. We all end up in a Cadillac. Any word on prints yet?"

"Andover's supposed to call me."

A priest began intoning, and the old altar boy in St. Onge emerged and he shut up. My eyes continued to rove, looking at faces and wondering if their owners felt the ambivalence I did. Once in awhile, without trying not to, I checked Lauren's face.

Standing farther away, at the fringe of the crowd, were Castle's personal assistant and his chauffeur. In mourning garb they looked like damp, overfed crows.

"You know those two?" I whispered to St. Onge, nodding.

He squinted. "Yeah, I know them," he whispered back. "Oscar Loomis is the little guy with the big talk."

Loomis, okay.

"Used to be a nag-rider, but he found his skills paid more off-track. The missing link is named Kaboski. I think he went swimming after they drained the gene pool. Between them they got a sheet you could wind a corpse in."

"What were they up for?"

"What weren't they?"

"Could you be more general?"

"Shut up, will you? What're you, an atheist?"

By the time the ceremony ended, the rain had practically quit too. St. Onge began to circulate, shaking hands, doing what cops do. A lot of the job is visibility and knowing people who might be useful down the line. I took a pass on the festivities. I wanted to get hold of Ada. Yesterday when I had called her I had reached only her machine. I quit leaving messages after the third time.

On my way back to where I had parked I spotted the Trouble Twins leaning against a car which was in front of mine but was not theirs. They were probably going to ask me to sign the guestbook. Actually I had been hoping to ask them a few questions, perhaps over a beer. Seeing me, Loomis rocked onto the balls of his feet. The heavy guy—Kaboski—stood glumly still, watching me with cold, deep-set eyes. He had his hands in his coat pockets to keep from scraping them on the ground. The pockets bulged like sacks of onions.

I grinned winningly. "Here to do a few grave rubbings?"

"Wanna talk to you," Oscar Loomis said, stepping away from the car and coming over to block my path. He was wearing a stone gray fedora. Under the black coat if he didn't have a white tie on a dark shirt I was going to be disappointed. He said, "We heard you were at Mr. Castle's domicile the night he passed away."

"When I found him, he'd already cashed out," I said, returning the euphemism. "I squealed for the heat from there."

"Funny you were there at all."

"Funny you weren't," I said. "Castle wasn't paying you for your twinkling wit."

Loomis touched the scar tissue on his forehead. "That's another funny thing," he said. "I get a call that afternoon saying Mr. C. wants a business associate picked up at Logan—only when we fucking get there, there's no such party. You know anything about that?"

I frowned, remembering that the state police had confirmed the airport trip to the Andover detectives. "Castle called you?"

"The message service."

"You didn't confirm it?"

"We get messages all the time. What's it to you? I still wanna know what you were doing there."

"A case I'm working on. It has nothing to do with you."

"Yeah? Suppose I make it do with me."

"Come on," I said equably, "this isn't a day for hassles." I moved to go around him, but he barred me.

"I'm making it one," he said.

I sighed. "I bet you were tough in the third grade."

Kaboski, who had kept back, came forward in a ding-toed shuffle, like the punch-drunk boxers Anthony Quinn used to play, only he wasn't playing. He had his hands out of his pockets. I braced as he moved alongside Loomis.

"I don't like you, rat-ass," he said.

"There's a lot of that going around," I said. "Take two bullets and call me in the morning."

I started past them when Kaboski's furry fielder's mitt of a hand dropped on my shoulder. I pivoted, grabbed a thumb, and yanked it up in a come-along hold that had him tap-dancing in surprise. He tried to knee me, but I stomped on his other foot, rooting him to the ground with pain.

Loomis I had not accounted for, but I should have. He had the rod out in a second, aimed right at my face. It was a reaction as automatic as the twitching of a mule's ear to shoo a biting fly. The gun was no collector's item. It was a blue-black Saturday nighter, the sort they stamp out in case lots in some Florida factory. I could see its castings and knew it would be studded with rust on the bottom of the river a day after it punched a sloppy, lethal hole in someone's head. Mine maybe. I kept the big guy moon-walking, trying to put him between me and the gun, trying to think. Loomis was fidgeting like a kid who has to pee.

"I'm gonna pop you, sonuvabitch!"

"Smart," I said. "I'm dead and five hundred witnesses make you both pen pals the rest of your lives."

He wasn't stupid. He had done time before. He glanced toward where the funeral crowd was dispersing, drifting back to their vehicles. A flicker even passed across Kaboski's cold eyes as if back in there someone had discovered fire. The gun disappeared, and I let go of the thumb. Kaboski clamped hold of it with his other hand and began to massage it. The three of us stood there, breathing hard. In a moment the hearse eased by, big tires swishing on the wet pavement. We caught our reflections in the dark glass, like an intimation of mortality. When the other cars had gone, we had all quieted. I briefly considered my idea of buying them a beer, but I had had enough excitement for one day. I opened my car door. "Peace?" I said.

Oscar Loomis pointed a finger. "Screw peace. Sleep with the light on, Jack. I see you again, you're gonna wish I didn't."

"Alas," I said, "I was wrong. It *was* your twinkling wit."

26

WHEN I GOT BACK to the office, a man was leaving a message on my answering machine in a precise, dry voice. I picked up and asked him to hang on while I shut off the machine.

"This is Rasmussen," I said. "I didn't get your name, sir."

"Are you *Alex* Rasmussen?"

"Speaking."

"This is John Potter from the Immigration and Naturalization Service, Boston office. You mailed us a letter on Monday last, I believe."

I managed to recover enough from shock to confirm it. Five o'clock traffic on the X-way moved at warp speed compared to the government's customary pace in handling paperwork. "Thanks for calling."

"We take inquiries such as yours, which request data on recent immigrants, very seriously. Do you mind if I ask the reason for your request?"

"As I said in the letter, general information."

"I'm afraid I'm going to need more than that. My office is responsible for investigating possible instances of discrimination. I'd never authorize the release of information without knowing why it's wanted."

And I knew by his tone that he wouldn't. "Mr. Potter, I think you're going to find that those people I listed were victims of an extreme form of discrimination. All, or most of them," I said, "are dead."

"That's quite a serious claim, sir! Would you care to—" His rush of words grated to a halt. The crispness wilted from his voice. "I'm . . . I'm afraid I don't understand."

I filled him in briefly. I don't know if he took notes, or even believed me. He did not ask questions right away, so I said, "Can I get that information now?"

"I've already assembled it. I checked it first thing. Now, however, I think I had better check on *your* information."

He was careful, was Mr. Potter. Efficient. I thought of giving him Ed St. Onge's number but decided the timing was not good. Instead I offered Lieutenant Nate Rosenheck of the Houston Police. Potter said he would seek to verify my story, and if it was borne out, he would call me back.

"One other thing," I said. "Would there be photo documentation for any of those people as well?"

"As a matter of fact, I have a group portrait."

"Group?"

"The individuals you listed, with one exception—this man Khoy—all arrived in the U.S. on the same flight from a refugee camp in Thailand."

You could have knocked me over with a rice cake. "And Khoy wasn't in the group?"

"In March of 1986, those individuals landed at San Francisco Airport to start their new lives. I've got a copy of their arrival portrait right here. Khoy *is* in the photograph though."

"I thought you just said—"

"That he wasn't a new arrival. He was employed in

California by a local assistance organization, helping new people to get settled. Now, if you check out, Mr. Rasmussen, I can fax the photograph to you along with the other data."

He seemed genuinely astonished when I told him I did not have a fax machine. I said that when he got back to me I would drive to Boston and pick up the materials in person.

"You could save yourself a lot of aggravation with a fax machine," he told me.

"Yeah, well, it was either that or paper clips this month."

So what did it mean that Bhuntan Tran and six others killed in distant parts of the country had all come to America together? Had they shared one experience too many? Known something they should not have? Possessed something deadly?

I paced my little office, listening to the floor under the carpet creak, peering out the windows every few circuits. The sky was the dark, wet gray of an old chalkboard, and I kept looking up to see if any answers were written there, but school was out for summer. My mind fingered the antique jade my eyes had never seen. But that did not work somehow. Of the group, only one person apparently had any connection with jade. Suoheang Khoy.

I got the case file and sat at the desk and began jotting numbers. Two of the Californians had been killed last July, and the third in October. Six weeks later, in Seattle a man named Keang Or had been found shot to death. The second Texas killing had been on May 19, five weeks before Bhuntan Tran had died. Seven deaths in twelve months. It was not a figure that jumped out at you. In D.C. you got seven in five minutes. But . . .

182

The phone rang and I grabbed it. "Mr. Potter?"

"Who? Alex, what are you doing?"

It was Ada. "Hi. Waiting. Playing with figures."

"Hmm—like you were the other night?"

"Cute. Numbers only, but my math's lousy. I tried calling you yesterday."

"I know, I got my messages. I've been away. Now I keep wondering what a woman's got to do to get a little attention."

"You don't have to do anything."

"Meaning nothing will work?"

"Meaning nothing won't. Can you get away for a spin into Beantown if my call comes through?"

"I wish I could."

"I'll even rinse your tofu later," I said.

She laughed, but her voice sounded different. "The fact is, Alex, I'm still away."

"New York?"

"How did you know that?"

"Apples, beans—I've got food on my mind."

"I'm attending a conference, this refugee advisory group I'm part of. What's up, anyway? Have you learned something about Bhuntan's death?"

I did not want to miss John Potter's call, so I said maybe and told her I would fill her in later. We murmured parting words that had an awkward ring.

Potter did things by the book, but he did them. The call came at four-fifteen. Rosenheck had okayed me. Potter said he would have everything ready when I arrived.

27

⊗⊙⊗⊙⊗⊙⊗⊙

THERE ARE FEW things deader than a twenty-five-story federal building after hours. Traffic and more rain had hung me up, but now the rain had stopped and Government Plaza had a nickel sheen that caught the rays of a brightening sky. The main entrance to the lobby was locked, so I wandered around outside for a few minutes checking doors before I noticed a cleaning van drawn up to the building. Two men were bulldogging a floor-stripping machine out of the back of the van. A uniformed GSA cop stood by, holding open a glass door. I told him I was expected by Mr. Potter.

"Your name?"

I told him.

"He done axed me you been in. You just missed him." The cop pointed in the direction of the ramp to the underground garage. "Might still catch him if you hustle."

My footsteps echoed as I descended the ramp. Gasoline spills made colorful splotches on the wet concrete, like small pieces of a rainbow that had fallen and been run over and was trying to reconstruct itself. When I entered the garage I paused. The place was mostly deserted, lit with yellow halogen lamps. By the far wall I spotted a man unlocking a gray Aries two-door. He had his arms full with a briefcase, folders and a raincoat, and when he had nudged open the door with his knee, he chunked everything onto the front seat. I started moving his way. He heard me and jerked around, the light from the lamps spilling off his spectacle lenses.

"Mr. Potter?"

He was middle-aged, his bushy eyebrows bunched with apprehension. People got mugged in parking garages, and worse. "Yes?"

"I'm Rasmussen."

He relaxed then, and waited for me. "I wasn't sure you'd make it," he said.

He had a plain face with hair like Harris tweed and watery brown eyes behind the Clark Kent glasses. We shook hands and he reached into the car and got a large brown envelope with a government frank in one corner. "Here's what you're after, along with the photograph."

I slipped the picture out and looked at it. "I marked who's who on the back," Potter said. "The quality isn't the greatest."

It wasn't, the picture having been photocopied and sent over the wire to INS's fax machine. Still, the faces were discernible. Mostly they looked tired and uncertain, but grateful too. Suoheang Khoy stood on the end at the left, a handsome man, unexpectedly tall. Unlike the others, he wore American clothes, the sleeves of his U Cal sweatshirt pushed to the elbows on thin arms. I didn't see any tattoos. I slid the sheet back into the envelope.

"I appreciate what you've done," I told Potter.

"Perhaps it's mutual. You won't explain anything more?"

"Later, maybe, if I can."

He fiddled with his car keys. "I apologize if I sounded

uninterested on the phone earlier. I'm not. What you've already told me, Mr. Rasmussen, is serious business. The fact is I admire the pluck of people who come here to start a new life. If that's what they truly want, it's good for the country. I despair some days of America's making it. I don't know, there's idiocy loose in the land, too much of it right up at the top. But . . ." he frowned, "this is still the best darn show in the world. If there's any other way I can help, I hope you'll ask."

I thanked him and he gave me a phone number that he promised would get me past the tape loops to him.

It was six-fifteen when I headed for the artery, but as I waited for a traffic light near the base of the on-ramp, I had second thoughts. For as far as I could see, in both directions, the lanes were plugged with traffic. At various points I could make out the twitchy flicker of a blue-and-white struggling through the mass. Deciding against injecting myself into that, I climbed down into the tunnel under Boston Harbor and headed for Logan Airport. The traffic was not much thinner and the air was life-threatening, but the run was shorter.

I stashed the car in central parking, a vast structure out of Dante and Hieronymus Bosch, with sprawling decks of concrete held up by squat pillars, like color-coded circles in Hell. I got yellow H and hoofed across an overpass to the terminal. I found the wing where the auto rental agencies had their booths. The city directory listed as many rental places as roach exterminators, half the names starting with *A* and climbing all over each other to be first in the listings. I figured the firms with branches at the airport were my best bet. With a one-man gumshoe operation you're playing percentages. *Exhaustive* is not in your dictionary; *exhausted* is.

To a one, the agencies seemed to be manned (I don't

know how else to say it) by young women with Breck hair-dos and the graciousness of Stepford wives. Invoking my tenuous link with the Lowell PD, I gave them Khoy's name and, in a couple of instances, showed the picture, asking about rentals going back three weeks. It almost never works, but I wanted at least to cross the question off the list. The idea was that if Khoy was the killer and had been working his way east, he might have flown in. The report of a small white car on Prather Street the night before Tran died was the only wedge I had.

Fortunately computers have made this kind of question easy to answer, and the answer I kept getting started to sound like an echo. "No, sir, I'm sorry, nothing for that spelling or anything close. Would it be under another name, sir?"

I didn't know. Changing names made sense only if someone was looking for you and you did not want to be found. For all I knew, Khoy had come here by train, bus, automobile, or thumb. Or he had not come at all. Maybe he was dead. I could almost empathize. After you fished a long spell without a nibble, you reeled in and changed bait. I got a cup of coffee and sat in the main concourse, watching people drag suitcases by like stubborn pets. A Rastafarian, with a custodian's cap perched atop his dreadlocks like a small tent beset by snakes, emptied ash-trays, the kind where you pressed a button and the butts dropped into a stainless steel canister below, which he dumped into his wheeled barrel, all done to a private reg-gae beat. Our eyes met and he gave me a stoned smile, which I toasted with my cup. He had his sacrament, I had mine. When the caffeine kicked in, I deposited the cup in his barrel, visited the washroom in preparation for the trek home, and blazed my way back to yellow H.

The logjam on the city side had vanished as neatly as if

someone had poked a big button and the ground had opened to let the traffic fall through. I wheeled north on 93 with nary a stomp on the brake. The clouds had broken, and the last of daylight was slanting through inspirationally. I tuned in the Sox, letting my mind fray out. Clemens had taken a break from shaking down kids who were asking for his autograph and was earning a piece of his ridiculous salary. He had six strikeouts after three and a half innings. It must be nice to be that good at something, I thought. Like a Gretzky or Navratilova or Michael Jordan. Or a John Potter. The way the Tran investigation was moving, I was not going to win any sleuthing prizes. Which needled me back to mulling. I shut the game off. The western horizon was ablaze with the sunset, and I moved with the other traffic toward it, like moths drawn to some final conflagration.

At the office I had a message to call someone about a problem a condominium association was having with its property manager. I put it on the blotter for the morning. I fished the business card for the Haskell and MacKay Gallery out of my wallet. Another woman answered but put Syd Keyes on without asking who was calling. Just as well; Ms. Keyes apparently still had me figured for the Castle killing. It took me awhile, but she was a smart enough cookie to agree that I would not be free and phoning if the police felt the same way. I reminded her that she had mentioned she kept evening hours by appointment. "Can I make one for tonight?"

She was silent a moment, then I told her what I needed. I thought I heard a snide little purr in her voice when she asked if I could be there in forty minutes.

I locked up and hiked across Kearney Square to the *Sun*. Bob Whitaker was off, so I wrote a note for him and sealed it in the brown government envelope with the faxed photograph and printed Bob's name on the outside. The receptionist promised it would be on the photo department desk waiting for him when he got in for his shift at seven the next morning.

Haskell and MacKay had a CLOSED sign in the window. No need for Sorry We Missed You, Please Call Again; if you did, you did. I knocked and after a minute Syd Keyes peered through the glass, then unlocked the door. I was wrinkled from rain and driving, and running a few hours behind my next shave, but I could not gauge how far wanting I was in the woman's cool appraisal. Evidently the notion that I was a killer was gone, at least. Maybe she had checked my Dun and Bradstreet. What I did know was that late hours did not mar her finish at all. The burnished-oak hair swooped smoothly, softening the patrician planes of her face. Her crimson lips gleamed. She relocked the door, and I trailed her across the big oriental rug.

"Would you care for some sherry?" she asked.

I said I didn't mind and she poured. Amontillado. It went with the objets d'art: the table with its tooled-leather-inlay top and the Tiffany lamp and the French telephone. An antique chessboard had been added, carved ebony and ivory pieces arranged on the sides near which we settled facing one another.

"So, what did you want to know about the Stewart fortune?" she asked, her breath misting the rim of the crystal glass poised before her lips.

"Whatever you can tell me."

Some of it I knew already from Ada, the rest was news. The family seemed to have inherited its seed money from

189

King Solomon, but Charles Blaine Stewart had turned it to Big Money with his clipper ships. His descendants had expanded into investments and real estate. With the generation of Ada's father, however, the old Scottish drive had lost momentum, and with Ada and her brother it had hit an abutment.

"The brother, Chad, took up anthropology," Syd Keyes said with dramatic distaste. "The last thing I knew, he was in Africa someplace, or South America. Living among primitives."

"Like Ada," I said.

She gave me an arch look. "You have to admit, to turn one's back on that kind of destiny is both irresponsible and rash."

"At least."

"And to compound irresponsibility the way Ada did . . ."

She paused, checking me closely to see how much I knew. I took a shot. "With her marriage."

"Her father disapproved, of course. Ada's parents had been the example of where that kind of marriage usually goes. They'd divorced when Ada and Chad were barely in their teens. So when Ada married—which must have seemed to flout him—he reacted."

I thought about Ada's overdue bills and her checkbook balance. "Cut off her inheritance?"

"What other leverage did he have? The family had long since lost physical control of her. Ada had grown up to be totally independent." Syd made it sound like a felony. "Of course, the inheritance could be restored someday, I suppose. That could be dangled like a carrot. God knows there's more money than her parents could have squandered. But any reinstatement would have to be at Ada's initiation, and when I remember that little girl who refused to come down out of the beech tree . . . well, I'm doubtful."

She angled her glass, gazing at the amber liquid as if it contained all the important answers to life—which is to say the ones pertaining to money. I tasted mine, but it was only old Spanish wine.

"When you said her parents' marriage was 'that kind,' you meant the fact that her mother was Chinese?"

"And the daughter of a servant. But at least they married for love. In Ada's case I've heard it was neither love nor money. No one knows for sure, because it happened out West a number of years ago, and Ada never kept any ties to Andover—but the rumor was they married to avoid trouble."

"She was pregnant?"

"No. The trouble was his. I had no idea what kind before you called tonight, so I made a call of my own. I've got a reliable source who makes a hobby of keeping track of the old families. Ada knew the man from Berkeley. The trouble he was in was for drugs."

"He was arrested?"

"For cocaine. He was going to be deported. Ada married him to give him citizenship."

I don't know if my jaw fell open or not. "Do you know his name? Or what nationality he was?"

"Those particular details weren't available."

I sat there, letting it all sink in. In her cool voice, Sydney Keyes said, "Rasmussen, I've been making all the moves so far. You haven't told me what your interest in this is."

"I'm hoping to keep some people out of trouble."

"That's rather ambiguous. Even noble perhaps. Would it do any good to ask you to go on?"

"I can't. Sorry."

She sipped amontillado, her long fingers with their blood-red nails curled around the glass's thin stem, and I had a helpless feeling for Ada, an ugly feeling about myself for having done it this way. Sydney Keyes's eyes were on mine. I slid a chess piece forward, set my glass on the vacant square and stood up. "I think you've answered my questions. Thanks."

"You weren't . . . looking for anything else?" she asked in a voice that made the words tickle my underbelly.

"Nothing I can think of."

She lowered her eyes and smiled with faint disappointment, like a teacher brought to frustration by a dim pupil. She locked the door behind me.

28

❧❧❧❧❧❧❧❧

"JUST GETTING DONE," Bob Whitaker said from the doorway of the *Sun*'s darkroom. He pointed to a desk, where I saw a batch of black-and-whites. "Something to keep you occupied." I knew by the quiet way he said it that they were his personal work. He ducked back into the darkroom and shut the door. It was seven-thirty A.M.

The prints were of a girl whom it took me a few seconds to recognize as the young cashier at the Owl Diner. So they had gotten together after all. The shots had been taken around the city, though everything in the backgrounds was wisely understated, the camera having found its true subject in the girl. Without the cigarette-smoke pall and china-plate clatter of the Owl, there was just the radiance of her face, framed by the clocksprings of Botticelli hair. Both of them should be doing it for a living, I thought.

There was a second pile of photos on the desk, which I realized had been taken the previous day, at Joel Castle's burial. These too were Bob's own, not the official stuff the paper had used last night. I flipped through them. Crowd studies, character shots. The great American way of death.

"How's this?" Whitaker asked.

The print was still tacky from the fixer, and without a negative to work from, the clarity was not crisp, but the picture was a leap over what John Potter had handed me. Bob had cropped Suoheang Khoy from the group of refugees at San Francisco Airport, and he had enlarged the print. I studied Khoy's face with more scrutiny now.

"I did up half a dozen for you," he said. He never would have fished for my reaction to the other work he had let me see, but I gave it anyway. He took the praise modestly, though I sensed his pride. My opinion mattered to him, so I never offered it lightly. As he got the other prints of Khoy into an envelope, he said, "Who is he, anyway?"

"Nobody you'd want to know."

I drove with my four-window AC on. The sun was back in force: drier, hotter, baking tar and brick and the vinyl upholstery I sat on. On Lawrence Street someone had opened a hydrant and a multicolor flock of kids was sporting in the thick gout that washed flattened beer cans and trash toward the storm drains. At the DSS office the sunburned receptionist told me Ada had not been in today, would not be until tomorrow. I wanted to ask her if Ada was in New York, but the taste of last night was still on my tongue like dirt. She let me go back to Ada's cubicle, where I left one of the prints face-down on her desk with a yellow stickum note asking her to call me as soon as she got back.

On the chance of catching St. Onge, I drove down to JFK Civic Center, where the locust pods hung limp and wasted-looking in the heat. I pulled into the lane behind the library and the police station, past a buzzing

Dumpster to where I could scope the window of Ed's office. The lights were off, the door closed. As I was about to back out, Gus Deemys and a man I did not recognize came out of the station, heading for a car. As always Deemys was immaculate, two-tone shoes, his snappy attire so wrinkle-free I could almost picture him sitting at his desk in his underwear until the intercom tipped him, then bustling into his clothes. I called to him.

He stopped and squinted. "Rasmussen," he said, making it a long slow sound. The guy with him was looking too, as if putting a face to a name he had heard.

"Seen St. Onge?" I said.

Ignoring the question, Deemys strolled a few steps nearer, but not too many. He had not forgotten our last encounter. Castle jokes would be in bad taste now, so he got inventive, pointing at the Dumpster. "Looking for lunch?"

I thought about just giving him the photo of Khoy to give to St. Onge, but I was tired of explanations. I put the car in reverse and slowly backed up.

"You can eat shit, man," Deemys called, growing brave.

I stopped and turned to meet his gaze. "What'll I do when I get to your bones, Gus?"

"Come out here and say that," he said.

I put the car in park and got out and shut my door. I walked over and stopped. "Here I am," I said.

His feet shifted, but he didn't take the shot—as I had known he wouldn't. Guys like him get their bravery from groups. The clothes were his way of telling the world to keep its distance. Shaking his head, muttering something too low to hear, he headed for the parking lot. The other guy followed. Big man, Rasmussen, I told myself, feeling diminished by cheap victory, withered all of a sudden by the heat. How long would it go on, this undeclared war? Attrition, with the occasional skirmish. Wouldn't life be easier someplace else?

I crumpled that idea fast and pitched it away. This was my territory. I got in my car. I backed out of the lane and drove away.

From my office I left a phone message for St. Onge to call me. I spread the Tran case notes on my desk and sat there in a funk. Information overload. It was the antithesis of boredom, yet in its effect it was the same: a dulling of the mind, a glazing of the eyes, a vast indifference to the world at large. The Sunday newspaper could do it, or a visit to a large museum. I was feeling it now. There were too many loose threads, and somehow the one I was most interested in tying up was the one which spooked me a little too. I needed to speak with Ada.

I might have let it ride. I might have called on George Dickel. But sometimes doing the little task when the big one is weighing on you restores balance. I returned the call I had received on the condominium matter. The number had a New Hampshire area code.

"Artificial Intelligence," a young woman said.

"Some days I think so too," I winged it.

"Sorry?"

I gave her my name and glanced at the note. "Karen Dubay, please."

The next voice was older. "Hi. Thanks for calling back. I wasn't sure of the protocol. I got your name out of the book. I've never dealt with an investigator before."

"This is a first for me, too. Artificial intelligence?"

She laughed. She was with a high-tech project, she said. Hush hush. On the home front, she went on, she was a trustee of her condo association in Nashua, a small one, ten units, which had self-managed for a few years before deciding to hire a pro. Now, after six months, they suspected the manager was skimming their accounts.

"Do you have evidence?" I asked.

She didn't. Mostly it was a vague unease that had them all nervous. Lately the manager was not returning calls, and they had just learned that his P.O. box hadn't been cleared in two weeks. I got details and said I would be in touch. I made a few calls and by leaning on the manager's message service got the name of a relative. That earned me the news that the manager had been in an accident while on vacation and was in a hospital in Denver. I called the hospital to discover the man was in guarded but stable condition, expected to recover—slowly. I did not talk with him. Next I contacted his bonding agency and explained the situation. The person I spoke to gave me a profile of the manager as an honest guy who unfortunately kept slipshod accounts. The agent agreed to meet with the condo trustees to reassure them. I called Ms. Dubay again and gave her the score.

"I'm amazed at what you've learned so quickly," she said.

"It's all there for the asking. The good news is your money's safe. The bad news is that for all practical purposes you don't have a manager."

"What would you advise us to do?"

"You're not buying advice," I said, "but your contract does call for thirty days' written notice. If you're unhappy, buy his month and can him and go back to running the show yourselves, or get someone else. At any rate, meet with the agent and see what he says."

She thanked me excessively, and when we had talked

fee she thanked me some more. How much are you going to sell a half hour of phone hassling for? "You can send the bill to me," she said.

"You won't forward it to the manager?"

After I hung up I could not help mulling Pascal's quip about the world's problems coming from man's inability to sit quietly in a room. I was saved by the bell.

"Hello, Mr. Rasmussen? This is Walt."

The voice was familiar but different somehow. "Walt."

"Rittle," he said.

"Got you, Walt. What's up?"

"I'd like to see you if I could." I realized what sounded different: the exuberance was gone. He sounded like he was talking so no one would overhear him.

"All right."

"Is twenty minutes too soon? At your office?"

"It's fine. What's it about, Walt?" I asked, but he had already hung up.

29

Ⓞ⦿⦿⦿⦿⦿⦿

TWENTY MINUTES was not soon enough. I was pacing by the elevator when the door slid open and Rittle stepped out onto the worn carpet, looking as nervous as I felt. I jumped on him. "What's going on? Where's Ada?"

The soft brown eyes behind his glasses blinked up at me in puzzlement. "She's in New York, isn't she?"

"Oh . . . yeah."

"She's taking a late flight back, I thought."

"So what's this about?"

"Well, I saw the note and—"

"Note?"

"Yeah . . . sorry."

It was a sitcom script. We were on different pages together. "What note?" I said.

"The stickum you left on Ada's desk. I looked at the photograph."

I relaxed a little; he wasn't here about Ada.

"Alex," he said, "I think I may have seen him."

"Khoy?"

"Is that his name?"

"Yes. Where'd you see him?"

He rubbed at his arms, bare in the blue Izod shirt he

had on. "Here in town, yesterday. I couldn't talk freely back in the office just now, on account of client confidentiality." He glanced toward the lawyer's door where a murmur of voices was coming through. I motioned him through my waiting room into my office, gestured to a chair and took my own.

"Has Khoy been a client?" I asked.

"No, no. I'd never seen him before yesterday. I was visiting a family over on Broadway. I think I passed him in a tenement stairway, just for a moment. He was going upstairs. I didn't think twice on it, but when I saw your photograph . . ."

I took another copy out of the batch Bob Whitaker had given me. "Is that him?"

Rittle studied the picture, angling it to catch the sunlight. He adjusted his glasses and breathed in and out deliberately through his nose several times. "The staircase was dim. But when you've worked with people a long time, you notice a lot of particularity in them. I got so's I used to see it with the Montagnards in Nam. I see it now with Cambodians." He touched the glossy face. "The eyes are similar. The shape of the face. I'm pretty sure. Though the person I saw looks older."

"He'd be close to four years older than that," I said.

"He was . . . harder too. Toughened. What's he done?"

I hesitated; but Rittle had come to me voluntarily. I owed him. "He might've murdered several people, including Bhuntan Tran."

"Jeezum."

"Yeah."

He swallowed, took another peek at the photo, then set it on the desk. "Shouldn't we go to the police?"

I found myself wishing I had spoken to St. Onge. "If the person you saw isn't him, how do you think he and the

200

other people there will take a lot of cops in riot guns and flak vests?"

Walt was rubbing again at his arms, lightly freckled under the sandy hair. "I wish I could be more certain, but I had just that one glance as he went up the stairs."

"What's up there?" I asked.

"Apartment, I guess."

If it was Khoy, he would have to know he was being sought. Maybe he was already gone. "Can you show me the building?"

As Rittle went out to get the elevator, I stayed behind a moment. I unlocked the bottom drawer of my file cabinet and got out the Masterpiece. The walnut grips smelled faintly of linseed oil. I swung the cylinder open and checked the full load, then slipped the .38 into the side pocket of my jacket. It was not the best way to carry, but I did not want to advertise to Rittle by taking time for the holster.

We took Walt's pickup, a little blue Isuzu with a trailer hitch with a faded yellow tennis ball over the ball tow. The cab was air-conditioned, but I felt myself sweating. On Broadway we drove past wooden tenements with clothes-lines running across the porches, flapping sheets and tube socks and Day-Glo shirts. He indicated a door and drove beyond and parked. The place was a sagging multi-unit done in a faded gray that would chalk off on your eyeballs if you looked too long. Someone had ripped an ancient heating system out of one of the basements, leaving ducts and casings heaped at the curb like a body pile after a robot war.

"You want to wait here?" I said.

Walt's Adam's apple bobbled like a soft-boiled egg. "I reckon I'll have to show you."

On the scabbing clapboards outside the door was an

array of mailboxes, each with a little padlock attached to keep the welfare checks from walking. The security lock on the door looked like it had quit the first time the cops knocked with a sledgehammer. The door swung into a dingy hall lit only by the plank of daylight that fell through the open doorway. I shut the door, and we let our eyes adjust, the ragged wainscoting and graffiti on the walls coming slowly into view. We did not have to wait for the smell. It was an amalgam of garbage, dry rot, grungy carpet, and Third World cuisine. I looked at Rittle, and he pointed. "Fourth floor," he said quietly.

"Last chance," I said.

He drew a deep breath. "I've got to satisfy myself now."

I led. From behind doors on the landings came music and raised voices, none of it in languages I wanted to know. Starting on the second floor, there were dim lights in overhead fixtures filled with the husks of fossil bugs. On the third floor I began noticing the little embossed plastic strips. PLEASE SHUT THE DOWNSTAIRS DOOR, and NO RUBBISH IN HALLWAY.

"This is where I passed him," Rittle said. "He went up there."

We climbed the final flight of steps. NO BICYCLES OR SHOPPING CARTS ON LANDINGS, advised another strip. The landlord must have got a tape writer with his tax refund check; he definitely wasn't going broke on building maintenance. Rittle showed me a door, battered wood like the others, with a stick-on number 12 on it. Piled next to the wall just beyond it were several collapsible cardboard inserts of the kind that come in wine cartons.

"Must've been a party," Rittle whispered.

"There'd be bottles," I whispered back; it was catching. "Where's the first place you go to get empty boxes?"

"Oh, yeah. Then somebody moved?"

"Looks like it." I laid my ear to the closed door. No sounds came from the other side. Reaching into my pocket and fitting my hand to the walnut grip of the Masterpiece, I put the other hand to work knocking. Behind me Rittle was doing a nervous little dance.

Surprise! There was no response.

That business on TV about jiggling a safety pin in the lock and "open sesame!" is a crock. Most decent locks are resistant to anyone but a locksmith, or a man with a hammer. I was neither. This lock felt like a deadbolt.

"Maybe the landlord lives in the building," Rittle said.

"Don't make jokes."

There was a gap under the door you could have rolled a baseball through. As I tried to figure a way to make it work, Walt got down on the cigarette-burned linoleum and peered under.

"Hey, Alex—got a pen?"

I gave him one, and he used it to slide out a key. I used the key on the lock.

"And I wanted you to stay in the car," I said.

He gave a shaky smile.

The apartment was stifling, and vacant—newly vacant, I judged. I didn't break my neck looking for the last month's rent or a forwarding address.

PLEASE TURN OFF LITES WHEN NOT IN USE, a sign urged. I used them. The place had a few sticks of furniture, the kind acquired by getting out ahead of the city rubbish fleet. We walked through four box-like rooms, moving slowly, but in the heat it was enough to have our sweat plopping onto the linoleum. The dripping sound I started hearing, though, was coming from the bathroom.

A stained plastic shower curtain was drawn across the

tub. Too many scenes from movies flickered through my mind. Rittle must have seen the same movies. We exchanged a look. He stepped back, and I yanked the curtain aside.

We gazed into an empty tub, scummed like the hull of a boat in Boston Harbor. *Drip . . . drip . . . drip* said the faucet. DO NOT THROW OBJECTS IN TOYLET, said a sign. "Whew," said Walt Rittle.

In the kitchen I gave up and opened a window. Whoever had lived in the apartment last had never really settled in. There was scant sign of life at all if you didn't notice the dried seeds of rice and a few petrified bean sprouts that the roaches had not carried off. In a straw wastebasket I pulled out from under the sink, there was a copy of yesterday's *Sun*. It was folded-open to the account of the Castle funeral. Rittle looked at it over my shoulder. "Isn't that the guy who was killed in his house in Andover?"

"Shot in the back of the head. Like Tran."

"Jeezum."

The news set Rittle dancing again, watching the door, eager to be gone. I stood by the sink, figuring. We could learn where the landlord was, get hold of him and find out who his late tenant had been; but there was little chance the name would be Khoy. If he had in fact been here, had killed those others in Texas and California, he would be five aliases away now. Suppositions. John Potter had linked the victims for me, but there was still no clear evidence or motive to tie the killings together. Those could come later. As we stood there, burning gray matter, someone was laying down tracks. I needed to find out who.

There was nothing else in the wastebasket but some dust and a shiny strand of metallic cellophane. We locked

204

the unit and pushed the key back under the door. Two floors down I got Rittle to knock on the door of the apartment belonging to his welfare client. A very dark man wearing a red, black and green knitted hat answered. He recognized Rittle and flashed a smile. "Mr. Walt," he said in an accent that explained the hat and the ebony skin, "do come in."

Rittle addressed the man as Joseph, said I was his colleague, and asked if I could use the telephone. Joseph seemed honored by the request. He led me in past a smiling family lineup.

St. Onge was not in. I asked the desk officer his name. Patrolman McGroarty. It rang no bells, and I hoped mine didn't either. Very briefly I urged him to notify the state police to put on an alert at Logan Airport and the train and bus stations for Suoheang Khoy. I told him there was an outstanding California warrant on Khoy for parole violation—just to give paper weight to my request—then added what I suspected Khoy of having done and gave the best description I could manage. McGroarty took the information without a lot of nuisance questions.

When we got into the hallway, Rittle said, "Joseph claims the man who rented unit twelve was Asian. He was there less than a month. It was news to Joseph the guy had moved out."

Downstairs in the foyer of the building something on the carpet winked in the sunlight as we opened the door, and I stooped and picked up a strand of cellophane tinsel. I glanced back up the stairway, thinking about icicles in July.

30

ⓞⓢⓞⓢⓞⓢⓞⓢⓞ

Funny what the mind will hang
onto. There is a place up there like the junk drawer, only
you cannot always find what you want, because there is no
inventory list. Sometimes, though, you are surprised.

It was four o'clock. An accident on one of the bridges
had traffic snarled. Cutting cross-grain to police headquarters was going to mean time, and more time I did not
want to fritter away on talk once we got there. Instead I
directed Rittle into the flow, down Market Street, right
onto Central, thinking as we went. Another right on Middlesex, past the boardinghouses and barrooms, missions
and shelters. In front of the bar where I had paid the
blackmailer's stoned woman for pictures of the politician's
naked girl, a group of men stood smoking and passing a
paper bag, waiting for Godot. I pointed out the cratered
side road next to a big lot behind chain-link fence. At the
end we turned into a cobblestone street between mill
buildings. Some of the mills were operational, but most
were defunct, or turned to purposes other than what, a
century and a half ago, they had been designed for. In the
deep shade, puddles from yesterday's rain were the color
of an old penny. Walt swamped through one, pumped the
brakes, and drove on.

At the second of two enclosed connecting ways that ran

overhead between buildings, I held my hand up. I was not sure which building I wanted, but it was here somewhere. We went over a low curb and down rutted dirt toward a clump of sumac. Among weeds and hills of broken brick lay discarded appliances and dead automobiles. Rust in piece. When I told Walt to stop, he asked the question with his eyebrows.

"That used to be Hamilton Textiles," I said, nodding at the building ahead. "These days it's storage. Remember when you were a kid and the Christmas decorations were kept in the attic?"

"Not sure I'm with you," Rittle said.

"That's the city's attic."

He frowned. He still wasn't with me. "You think this guy came here?"

From my inside jacket pocket I tweezed out the strand of tinsel I had found in the apartment hallway on Broadway, which was like the one in the wastebasket in apartment twelve. "You know anywhere else you'd pick this up this time of year?"

"Jeezum," Rittle said, but as he did, I felt my idea dwindle, lost in the patchwork of hunches I had been stitching together and the scale of the edifice before us. It was a vast and dilapidated building of dirty brick. The windows that were not stuffed with rags were coated with grime that had begun to accumulate when Roosevelt was president—*Teddy* Roosevelt. I must have read somewhere that all the holiday trappings which bloomed on city lampposts and public buildings before Thanksgiving dinner was fairly digested were kept there during the rest of the year.

Well, I had had sillier ideas; this was no time to begin rejecting them on that basis. I dropped the strand of tinsel into the ashtray.

We were partly hidden by the sumac. This time I did

not suggest that Walt wait in the car. I *told* him. Tension had frozen the convivial softness of his face, but it was not panicky fear; not if he had been with the 82nd Airborne. "I want you to keep an eye on that gate over there," I said. "Anyone interesting comes out, take notes."

I climbed from the pickup and walked toward a big archway in the facade that was partly barred by rusty iron gates which opened in from both sides, like the portcullis of a Norman fortress. It was the kind of gate that had locked out workers a hundred years ago when the owners sent the yard bulls in with truncheons, and blood had spilled. A memory stirred, of another time I had gone into the courtyard of an abandoned mill, that time to keep a midnight appointment. I touched the shape of my .38 in my coat pocket, but for the moment the only thing I drew was a steadying breath. I slipped sideways through the opening and walked into an enclosure hip-deep in summer weeds that snatched at my pantlegs like small warning hands. A faint trail told me a vehicle had passed through not long before, but I was not left to wonder how long. In the courtyard, on an apron of broken asphalt, sat a little Ford GT, white with white sport wheelcovers. There was an Alamo rental sticker on the rear bumper. Damn. I had not remembered the Alamo.

The car was not locked, but I gave the interior only a cursory look through the dusty driver's-side window. A few wrinkled shirts on the back seat, the flashy kind that go with heavy gold chains and bad taste. On the hump where the transmission ran under the gear shift I saw what could have been the shed skin of a garter snake but wasn't. It was a plastic tube that rocks of crack came in. Someone was getting sloppy. Which meant I had better not.

The mill door was unlocked, the hasp having been jimmied loose. This was getting too easy. I opened the door as quietly as you can a 150-year-old door built to Frankenstein scale. I went inside and closed the door behind me.

There were enough uncovered windows high in the wall at my back so that daylight fed through in sulfur-stained shafts, diffusing into the gloom, making the place an eerie cathedral. I was able to see the cutout sleighs and reindeer, snowflakes and snowmen—and there were probably snowwomen too: the government would require it. Ahead I saw a big pointy star fashioned from sheet metal painted gold and realized it was the one that graced the front of city hall each December.

The high ceiling was supported on wood posts thicker than phone poles, and there were rusty stanchions where cogs once had been mounted and overhead hangers where drive belts had run, empty now except for the nests that birds had built with twigs, and bits of straw, and shimmery tinsel.

Along the far wall, running the length of the room and twenty feet above the floor that I was on, was a loft. Behind the railing, I could see reels of electrical wire and the cables that DPW crews strung across the city streets with plastic bells and wreaths. I listened and did not hear Nat King Cole, or any other sound.

But I saw footprints. A trail of them in the dust led to the stairs on the right. Time for the Smith & Wesson. I started to climb, trying to be quiet. I might as well have tried to look like Mel Gibson. The stairs creaked and groaned with each step.

On the upper level I picked my way among the snaking wires and cable reels. There were actually two sets of footprints, I realized now. My own prints were the third. The person who had left one of the other sets sat on the floor, upright against a crate, back to me so I could see only a bleached tangle of hair. I stepped nearer.

It was the woman who had delivered the blackmail photos for Tony Rossi. The eight A.M. party girl. Her name had vanished from my memory, though that did not matter, because I wasn't going to use it anytime soon. No one was.

I squatted and set the .38 on the floor next to my knee. I nudged her arm. She was as stiff as a department store mannequin. I could not gauge how long she had been dead, but it had not been too long. There was no decay that I could detect, no odor getting past the wrinkled sleeveless blouse and the soiled jeans and the dust drifting in my nostrils. I saw no blood, no signs of wounds or injury.

Bending closer I noticed a few delicate white crumbs above her upper lip, like frost crystals. It was not hard to figure. When you were as far gone as she had seemed the other time I had seen her, you weren't fussy about where or with whom you partied. Maybe she never delivered the blackmail money. More likely Rossi had given her a few bucks, then taken his lion's share and split for some new enterprise, while she sank her cash into the highest-risk investment there is.

The looks she had had were gone now in the swollen tissues of her cheeks, snuffed from the dull, dented eyes, and I felt a wrench of regret that I had not extended more of a hand when I had seen her going down that week-ago morning in the barroom.

I didn't have time to indulge the sentiment. A gunshot shattered the stillness and tore a knot out of the floor a yard from my left knee.

I rolled backwards, looking for something to get behind. There was nothing close. A crouched figure lurched from behind a wall of crates.

"*Stop!*" he screeched. He held a small, shiny automatic pointed at me.

I didn't push it. He could not have missed me by the distance he had if he hadn't wanted to. I put my hands in view. Slowly I got up.

Rittle had been right: the face had put on years since the airport photo. It was a road map of hard travels on bad roads.

"I didn't kill her," Suoheang Khoy said in a tense voice. I did not move.

"I didn't kill her!"

"I know you didn't, Suoheang."

Khoy's eyes narrowed, then widened. He was agitated, full of nervous energy that wanted someplace to go. The automatic was jerking like a baton, flashing a bright reflection on the ceiling and walls. My own weapon lay on the floor near my right foot, as useful as a beanbag. I could almost see Khoy's mind trying to decide what came next. I gave him an option.

"She overdosed," I said. "You sold the jade and used the money for coke. Your addiction has taken over, man. You're on the run. You need help."

"I didn't kill her," he said again, more desperately.

"We've been there. What do you want to do?"

"Not *anyone*," he said, shuffling closer, adding something in a language I didn't know. I kept my hands up. Off to the left, far behind him, a sudden trapezoid of light caught my eye, then was gone. I realized what it had been. I did not look again. My heart was drumming a fast, even beat.

"What about Bhuntan Tran?" I asked.

211

"Bhuntan's dead!"

"That's right."

"He was my friend!"

"Is that why you went to see him the night before he was killed?"

The dish of Khoy's face filled with panic. He shouted some words I didn't know. I was pretty sure that his mind was taken over by the drugs. I was searching for my next stall when he must have sensed movement. He swung around, and we both saw Walt Rittle padding toward us fast in a crouch.

"Down!" I shouted to Rittle.

Khoy gave a spasm of words I didn't catch and bolted past the dead woman, blasting three more rounds as Rittle fell. Headed for the railing, Khoy wheeled and fired in my direction, but I was already rolling behind a crate, my hand on the Smith.

I banged off a shot and saw Khoy spin backwards, but he wasn't hit. My aim was wide. He had the automatic in both hands, crouching. Before either of us could fire again, a grumbling made the floor shake. Khoy's eyes darted, and we both saw a heavy cable reel rolling toward him. Rittle had shoved it. Panicked, Khoy emptied his gun, spraying rounds at the heavy drum, splintering wood, but it rolled on like a dump truck through daisies. At the last instant he tried to fend it off with his hands. The collision knocked him back. He hit the railing. The dry wood crackled with a sound like summer lightning.

There are no language barriers for a scream.

When I had scurried out of cover to peer down, I knew Khoy was never going to make a sound again. He had fallen onto the sheet metal star. Two points had gored through his back and come out his chest. I turned away.

Walt Rittle stirred among the boxes and crawled out shakily. I put my gun away. "It's over," I said. "You okay?"

He nodded. He got up slowly and adjusted his glasses. He edged to the shattered railing on Gumby legs. He gazed down for a moment, then backed away. His shirt was covered with dust and splinters, and a few strands of tinsel decorated his hair. He made no move to brush them off.

"You were supposed to be the outside man," I said with what I hoped was a grin. I hadn't been sorry to see him come through that door. "How'd you get there?"

"Climbed a fire escape. When I heard those gunshots, and you didn't come out . . . I got scared. I thought you might need me."

I held out a hand and he gripped it. "Thanks. Khoy wouldn't have been brought back alive. He was too far gone."

Gingerly Walt picked up a plastic bag of white powder that lay open on one of the crates. "Is this what I think it is?"

"Most likely." I nodded toward another crate. "Just a warning—there's a woman over there who's dead."

He recoiled. "Oh, jeezum. He killed her?"

"OD'd, I think. We better leave things for the cops to sort out."

He peered around, waiting maybe to feel steadiness return to his legs. I did not complain about the delay. After a few minutes we walked out together.

Walt seemed a little steadier and said he would wait with his truck while I hiked over to Middlesex Street and found a phone. I gave the message to the woman who answered and asked to have a cruiser and an ambulance sent. A directory hung on a chain in the booth. The shriveled book inside the hard plastic covers looked like it might have Alexander Graham Bell's number in it. I got Ada's number instead and called it but hung up when her answering machine came on.

There was already a cruiser in the outer yard and a pair of cops, one of each gender, when I got back. The male cop was standing with one foot on the shiny ball of Rittle's trailer hitch, notebook open on his knee, jotting notes. Walt was working to keep steady as he talked to them. In the distance a siren wailed. Deep in my mind a submerged perception moved, but I could not get it to surface. In a few minutes an ambulance arrived. We got the rusted gates open.

By the time dusk was falling, a host of black-and-whites and another ambulance occupied the courtyard, engines running, light-bars splashing the dark walls with circus colors. Cops aren't energy smart.

It was the wrong time of day in the wrong part of town for much of a crowd to gather. What spectators there were had shuffled over from bars and flophouses and stood among the weeds, perhaps dimly aware that one of their fraternity had bought a one-way ticket out of skid row. St. Onge showed up and went inside. When he emerged, he ordered the place sealed until floodlights could be brought in and he got back to head the investigation himself. He motioned for Rittle and me to come with him in his car. Walt gave the keys to his truck to a cop, who promised to park it on the street outside police headquarters.

Beyond an inexpressive grunt or two, St. Onge drove the unmarked Ford in silence. He stopped on Middlesex in front of a taproom with black plywood over the windows and a propped-open door and told us to come inside. The place was dim and aromatic, deserted except for a few drinkers mumbling to themselves over shot glasses. No one was drinking Harvey Wallbangers or Tequila Mockingbirds. Still following Ed's example, we sat at the bar. The bartender ran a careful hand over his pompadour and left it on the back of his neck, waiting. "Three whiskeys," St. Onge told him and threw down a five-dollar bill, glaring at Walt and me, daring us to object. We didn't.

The barman set up glasses and got a bottle, Old Thom if you believed the label. "You gents hear about those folks they found out back?" He clucked his tongue. "Terrible thing someone dies like that. What was it, gooks?"

"Pour them level," St. Onge said. He did not say another word until we got downtown.

31

AT JFK CIVIC CENTER the cops took my gun. They got Rittle in one room and me in another. They dispensed with the bright lights and stage-dressing third degree, but they had questions. Lots. Topping the list was why hadn't I gone to them with the photo of Khoy and the report that he was in town. Deemys, in a rare moment of largesse, admitted that I had been by that morning looking for St. Onge. Maybe I was just a smaller-bore threat to Deemys than Francis X. was. The Ogre stood by the door with his thick arms crossed, watching the show.

"You should've given us a call when you found the apartment," St. Onge said.

"And say what? Only a hundred-sixty shopping days till Christmas? A strand of tinsel would've gotten me a laugh."

It went on like that for awhile, then Droney pushed away from the wall and came over. The others fell silent. In the fluorescent light, the embroidery of blood vessels in Droney's cheeks was impressive. He said, "I'm still gauging how deep in the shit you are, Coin Op. Figure I already got you for criminal trespass and B and E. I find you interfered with the investigation, I'm gonna whack you with an obstruction charge so fast the fillings in your teeth'll rattle. Quote me."

I made a pretense of noting it on my palm. After awhile he stalked out. There were more questions, then the cops left the room to confer. St. Onge came back in alone.

"Rittle's story backed yours," he said.

"See?" I said. "Tell Droney."

"Droney makes noise. There's nothing on you and he knows it."

I wiped fingers across my brow and made a sidelong flinging motion with the hand. St. Onge said, "I thanked Rittle and told him he was free to go. You stay."

He got us Styrofoam cups of burnt coffee and took me down to his own office, where he parked a haunch on his desk, his eyes lidded against the curl of smoke from a Camel, and had me go over everything again. My gaze kept straying to the mountain meadow in the Sierra Club poster behind his desk. At last, even he seemed to tire of the questions. He sighed. "Finding corpses is getting to be a habit of yours," he said.

"I'd rather find money."

"Looks like you're going to. The Stewart woman must be into you for some long green."

"Am I free to walk?"

"Who's stopping you?"

My feet stayed where they were. St. Onge said, "Well?"

"Now we just wait for the red tape to arrange itself in neat ribbons and bows," I said.

"Got a different idea?"

I shrugged.

"Rasmussen."

I was still tentative on Khoy's link to Bhuntan Tran's death. I told him so.

"It's circumstantial," he granted. "But the coke computes. And maybe Khoy wanted the money he'd lent Tran to buy the house. Druggies get desperate enough, they get crazy. So we wait for ballistics on his weapon. The point is, I like Khoy for the Castle burn. That one's pretty straightforward."

"And that's the one that'll get headlines," I said.

For an instant, I thought he might come at me, or swear at me, at least. But he didn't. It was late. He took his time squashing the cigarette butt. "Yeah," he said, "that's the one."

Outside, I stood among the locust trees in the cooling dark and watched the traffic lights on the corner go through a few cycles. A Firebird with fat tires did some roadwork on Dutton. A pair of thirteen-year-old girls in tight jeans and spike heels walked by, practicing for when they grew up. St. Onge would smoke a cigarette, get another cup of coffee and call Leona to say he was going to be late, then he would go back to the crime scene and pester the techs. I figured on being in dreamland by then.

But when I had walked the long blocks to Kearney Square where my car was still parked behind number ten, I was wide awake.

The Victorian on Christian Hill was dark behind the screen of maples. Ada's Celica was not in the driveway. For the first time I realized I had been thinking about her all day. I wanted to say to her that we would find a way to make it all come up roses, or words to that effect. Not finding her at home now, I felt disappointment take a crisp bite out of my hope.

I was not ready for my apartment walls. I drove around the city, checking the pulse of the streets, killing time. Bars and self-serve gas stations, all-night quick marts and diners were the only places still open. As I waited for a traffic light, a woman in halter top and high shorts glanced my way. If vice picked her up, the blotter would call it common nightwalking. We were both out there in the wee hours, searching the streets for something. I had grown aware again of my vague earlier perception nagging me, some little jigsaw piece that did not have a corresponding gap in the big picture. Maybe it had to do with Suoheang Khoy's final acts. Like why hadn't he shot me when he had the chance? Why hang around the city in the first place? Some of the irrationality could be laid to the coke—perhaps he imagined he was safe, immune, superman. But did someone with that much blood on his head go down bluffing, trying to explain? Explain what?

On Thorndike I waited while a little yard-locomotive chugged a long train of cars past to an empty siding. It seemed an enormous labor. When the last freight car was gone and the crossing gate went up, I drove through with an idea.

Mine were the only wheels in the darkened lot behind the DSS building. I took a flashlight from the glovebox, locked my revolver in there, locked the car.

My hunch about the back door was right. Because it had swelled, it was hard to close all the way, so somebody had not quite managed the task. A few hard yanks and it quivered open. I didn't pause to wonder what I would have done if it hadn't.

I knew from past visits there was no electronic security—it's the kind of thing I notice. Human-service organizations are low rung on the public ladder, so there is little anyone would bother to steal. *State-of-the-art* here meant reconditioned office equipment passed down from the Sewer Commission. I flicked on the flashlight and located Ada's desk in the little cubicle in back.

I was not sure what I was looking for. I checked a file cabinet, desk drawers. Beside the computer was a plastic diskette box. I flipped through the disks, reading labels: correspondence, case reports belonging to Ada and other caseworkers, an unlabeled disk. I turned the machine on and put that disk in. When the machine had booted, I called up an index and began scrolling through lists of documents. One document name interested me, so I pulled it up on the screen. Nothing good. I tried a second and a third document. I yawned. As the files scrolled past, I yawned some more. Go home, I told myself. Getting caught here would be the thing Droney needed to hang me.

The last item in the index was a document with the simple title "X List." What the hell, one more, then I was out of there. I hit the keys.

My heartbeat quickened.

Names moved on the monitor screen.

Names I knew because I had sent a list of them to John Potter.

Names of the dead.

32

ⓔⓧⓔⓧⓔⓧⓔⓧⓔ

BY SEVEN A.M., showered and shaved, I broke starch on the last clean shirt in my dresser. I got a speck of blood on the collar from a razor nick as I knotted my tie. At quarter past I dialed her number. Her hello was thick with sleep.

"It's Rasmussen."

"Hi," she purred. "Goodness, it's early."

"Or late. I haven't been to bed yet. How are you?"

"Sleepy. I got in late myself." Her lips made a contented smacking sound. I could see her stretching, one arm behind her tousled head; maybe she had on the blue silk kimono. Then it caught her. "You haven't slept?"

I didn't think she had heard the news, but I asked anyway.

"No, what's going on?"

"Your former husband is dead." I let her bobble that one for a few seconds then tossed the next one. "He was killed in Lowell last night."

Her reaction was immediate, without time to be faked. "Oh, no. Oh my God, Alex." Then she did pause. I expected her to ask how I had made the connection, but she didn't. She knew I had, and that was enough. "Was he the one who . . . ?" She didn't finish.

"It appears that way. It's up to the police now. I want to see you."

"Of course. When?"

"I've got a few things to do," I said. "Ten o'clock, your office?"

"All right."

I went by the *Sun* offices. Bob Whitaker was out, but one of the other photographers let me look on the desk, and there I found the shots Bob had taken at the cemetery the day of Joel Castle's funeral. Yesterday, when I had looked at the pictures, my mind had been elsewhere—but not totally, I saw now as I scanned the faces. I put the pictures back and left.

There were two mobile news vans outside JFK Civic Center. They were illegally parked, but I'd bet they wouldn't get ticketed. As I headed inside, stepping over cables as thick as rattlesnakes, I glanced into a conference room and saw Droney smiling at reporters. He was wearing a man-of-the-year suit, and under the lights his shrewdly beaming face was pink as a boiled ham. What I heard of his statement declaring a close to the Castle murder case sounded as genuine as a major leaguer's postgame interview. I didn't listen long.

At the end of the corridor I knocked on St. Onge's door and went in. Ed was squinting into a round mirror perched on his file cabinet, a cigarette doing a Robert Mitchum droop from his lower lip as he mowed stubble with a cordless shaver. Magnified in the mirror, his nostrils looked like a snout of a double-barrel 12-gauge. I was not a bit surprised to find him still in yesterday's shirt.

"If they put you on camera," I said, "there's this thing they can do with a silk stocking over the lens."

"Bullshit. I feel sound as a dollar."

"Then I'd get to a hospital right away."

He gave it the response it deserved. When he finished shaving, he fingered his cheeks and throat, then put the shaver and the mirror in the file cabinet, shut the drawer and came over to his desk. He drew the last smoke out of the cigarette and crushed the stub. His eyes didn't widen much beyond the squint. He used a bottle of Canoe he must have got in high school and patted some on. "So?" he said.

I rolled my head to indicate the doings down the hall. "How are things with the ribbons-and-bows detail?"

"Droney knows this'll be good for the rest of the week. He's right. I've already spoken with Rosen-face down there in Texas."

"Rosenheck."

"The pieces are starting to come in. When the ballistics report gets back, I think we'll tie Khoy and his weapon to the Tran hit, and probably the others."

"The dead blonde have any connection?" I asked, saying nothing about having met her once before.

"No. A wiggle-tail named Rita Girard. Used to strip at the Blue Moon and hook a little. She had a habit. Probably linked up with Khoy on account of his stash. Too bad, she was a good-looking head."

"Some people aren't to be trusted with the keys to the candy store. You find the jade?"

"We will. The little bastard had nearly ten bills in his pocket. Figure he fenced the stuff."

"I doubt it."

St. Onge gave me the look.

"That was old Chinese-carved jade," I said. "Nephrite, if it matters. Yunung-kash. More than likely the cash is what's left of his sale to Castle, the little that didn't go up his nose."

"Then he's got it ditched somewhere. His fingerprints place him at Castle's. It's a good bet he stole the jade back, iced Castle and was waiting to find another pigeon to sell to."

"You may be right," I said. "Yep, probably are. Well, I'll let you get back to the beautification project." I headed for the door.

I stopped. "Oh, yeah. Almost, forgot. Have you guys finished sniffing my gun?"

He dug it from a drawer in his desk and handed it over. "Anything else?" he said.

"Well, I was hoping the TV stations needed a presence for the six o'clock news, but I can see you and Francis X. have got everything covered."

He showed me his longest finger.

Back in my office I could have used my own phone and patience, but I didn't have all week. I found the number John Potter had told me would snip the barbwire at Immigration and Naturalization. He didn't answer himself, but someone willing to accept minimal explanation once I'd asked for Potter did. In about twenty seconds Potter was on the line. I told him how things stood, about the death of Khoy—which he had caught on the morning news—then I laid out the reason I'd really phoned. He gave himself a meditative span of silence then ran through the rudiments of a plan aloud. I was glad I had called him. He was my inside man, and he knew a few tricks. He said he would get back to me as soon as he could. I didn't press for a time. I knew he wouldn't take any longer than he had to.

Even with the tricks the minutes ticked by. It was going

on ten o'clock when he called back, quarter past by the time I got to DSS.

Ada had sounded tired when my call awakened her at seven-fifteen, but she was fully alert now. Her face was scrubbed and glowing. I couldn't tell if her eyes had shed tears. She had on the black skirt and pale pink blouse she'd been wearing the day we met, and that innately suspicious part of my brain wondered if she knew this too. Was there half mourning in her mood, and half joy?

She led me back to her cubicle. There was no door to close. "I heard all about it on the radio. You were right about Suoheang."

I nodded. "You were right about Bhuntan Tran."

"We both were. I have things to tell you, Alex." She was searching my face for something.

"Same here."

"There are reasons why I never told you about having been married, and about Suoheang. I honestly didn't think he was involved in any of this."

I shrugged.

"It's a long story," she said.

"Okay, but I want to see Walt first. Is he around?"

"Not yet."

"The excitement probably wore him out. You know where he lives?"

She found the address in a Rolodex file and wrote it on a yellow note square. As she gave it to me, she touched my hand. "This evening?"

"Sure," I told her.

At the doorway I turned. She looked at me. I was trying to think of something to make it easy; but that was a wheel you could turn all day and night and still find yourself where you started. I waved.

225

33

⊙⊙⊙⊙⊙⊙⊙⊙

THE ADDRESS WAS not familiar, though I knew it was off Rogers Street, a busy drag of car dealerships, drive-up banks, fast food and faster oil changes, all winking in the midday sun. I almost missed the turn. Businesses on the narrow road thinned quickly—an auto body shop, a fenced storage yard—and then it was dusty hardpan with tall bulrushes on one side, swampy woods on the other. Finally I saw a trailer park, a dozen decaying units scattered around a two-acre lot with a cluster of mailboxes at the entrance. The road went on to a cement plant, I knew, and a limestone quarry that had not been worked in years. It was full of standing water. I had swum there as a kid with Joey Costello. It was a long way from the glimmering pool in Andover.

Walt Rittle's pickup, hooked to a small flat-top camper, was beside the third trailer in, a rust-freckled beige and green affair with 1950s contours. Clumps of willow and tiger lilies crowded the cinderblock foundation. Everything was powdered with fine dust from the passage of cement mixers.

I rapped on an aluminum door beyond which came the twang of country and western music. Except for a chopped Harley missing a front wheel, there were no vehi-

226

cles at any of the neighboring trailers. One had an orange
FOR RENT sign on it, and in the yard of another a black
German shepherd on a cable-run barked at me. Even he
looked dusty. I knocked again and after a moment Walt
opened the door.

"Hey, Alex." No alligator this time. He was in brown
cords and a denim workshirt. "C'mon in. I've got the
AC on."

I had about two inches of headroom on the inside,
which consisted of woodgrain-panel walls and a brown
and gold chessboard floor of press-on linoleum squares. A
sofa in green and mustard tweed did double duty as a bed.
At the back end, to my right, a louvered door was closed
on what I guessed was the bathroom. At the front was an
open kitchenette with a small portable radio playing and a
light on over the butane stove. Otherwise the trailer was
dim and cool.

"How 'bout some iced tea?" Walt asked. "I just this
minute mixed a batch. Or I can fix you a bourbon. With a
little branch water?"

"Not out of that branch out there, I hope. No thanks," I
said.

"Coffee? You look tired."

"No."

"Well, set a spell. I'm not going to work till late today.
Figure I earned me a breather last night. We both of us
did. Sit down."

Out of uniform, he had downshifted into a casual, more
Southern persona. I sat on the day bed sofa. He moved
into the kitchenette and lowered the volume on the radio.
Coarse beige drapes hung open a few inches over a
screened jalousie window through which I could see the
tower of the cement plant and past that, through trees, the

227

flash of cars on 495. The window AC unit chugged away, browning out the power every few moments as it cycled up and down. Walt looked over from putting ice cubes into a large mason jar of tea. "So, how do you like my little place?"

"You rent?"

"Yep. Cheap."

"This used to be the Amazon jungle when I was a kid," I said. "That highway was just a smudge on some state DPW engineer's plat."

"Still is peaceful, except for the trucks, and the neighbor's pup. She'll hush up pretty quick." He dropped the empty ice tray in the sink and began stirring sugar into the tea.

"You giving notice when you go in today?" I asked.

He glanced sideways, puzzled a moment, then laughed. "Are we due for a fat reward from a grateful public?"

"I doubt it. But then I guess you've got all you'll ever need, huh?"

The rattling in the jar quit, but the soupy liquid went on swirling in a slow brown vortex. He was eyeing me quizzically. "What's this about?" he asked.

"About this much." I held forefinger and thumb an inch apart. "About almost pulling it off."

I was watching for the small changes, but I did not see them, and the thought crept into my mind: my connections were crossed. Too little sleep could do that. He poured tea into a tumbler and came into the main room. He pushed his glasses up with a finger. "I reckon I don't read you," he said.

"Ada said it days ago. Social work is a burnout job. People don't last long doing casework. She didn't mean you, of course. Ada thinks you're superman. We all did."

He set the glass of tea on a plastic parson's table at the end of the sofa and looked at me like I had been pan-frying in the sun. I felt leaden with exhaustion.

"Jeezum, Alex, I'm gettin' a mite riled here. Where you goin' with this?"

"All those years with the State Department," I said, "some of them as a relocation counselor in the Cambodian refugee camps in Thailand. That must've been heavy. Before that isn't quite clear, some kind of classified recon over there. You told me you were Airborne. You said you'd gotten to know Montagnards. That where you picked up the t'ai chi?"

"Is that what this is, man? Old war stories?" He tried a grin, but it did not go deep; his eyes didn't join in, and that's when I knew I was right. I kept going.

"You must've heard a lot of atrocity stories in the camps. I'd imagine that to get extra rice or medicine or maybe a chance to be out of there, the survivors of the Khmer Rouge were willing to trade most anything. Probably even old family treasures," I said. "Like jade."

He looked like the heat was getting to him too. He removed his glasses and pinched at the red groove they had left in the bridge of his nose. All at once his vitality seemed to fail him. He settled onto a chair near the door. On the radio a hillbilly vixen was singing about hangovers and heartbreak.

"This is kind of crazy," Walt said.

"No argument here." Outside, the neighbor's dog barked just to hear itself. "You must've needed a way to move the jade, since getting caught would've meant your job, and probably a stretch in a federal slam. What'd you do? Entrust the stones to someone coming Stateside?"

"Crazy," Walt said again, putting his glasses back on.

But it wasn't anymore. Last night, watching the locomotive tug its freight cars had prompted me to remember that when I had gone back to the courtyard at Hamilton Textiles, the tennis ball cover had been pulled off the trailer hitch on Rittle's truck. He had already been preparing to skip. "Maybe you laid the stones on one of the Cambodians who was getting out," I said. "Only he got cute and decided it was a better cut if he took it all."

I was inventing, off on details most likely, but the big pieces stacked up. I had worked on them most of the night. John Potter's phone calls that morning to the right places in the federal web had confirmed Rittle's military service and work overseas. Walt let me blow solo awhile, and I went on about how, when he had finally mustered out and come back to the world, he saw the way it was, so he set out to find whoever had crossed him. Or maybe he had assumed everyone in that one particular refugee group that got to California was in on the rip-off, so he started in Stockton and worked down the list.

"Really crazy," he said when I finished.

"I had my doubts too, until I saw the diskette at the DSS office listing the names of the Cambodians on the flight. I thought it was Ada's file at first, but then I knew it was yours, and that now you'd be moving on. Was the method of killing just inspiration? To scare them into confessing about the jade? Or were you looking to set somebody up? You probably didn't learn much. I doubt anyone but Khoy knew. He was in San Francisco doing outreach with new refugees then, but he'd already acquired a coke habit. In fact, he got busted for it. Ada knew him from Berkeley, so she married him to save him from being sent back as an undesirable. One of her human reclamation projects, I guess. She got cut off from her family's dough for it. Khoy would've needed money to fund his habit and his lifestyle, so the jade made sense."

Rittle glanced away as if he were going to go on denying everything. I was too tired for games. The cops could handle the rest of it. I turned to look for a telephone.

He moved with a quickness I should have remembered from that night in Lauren's kitchen. His right foot slammed into the outside of my knee, dropping me onto the sofa. He covered the few steps to the door in an instant and yanked it open, so I had to wince against the blaze of pain and sunlight to see that he wasn't bolting. Someone else was there. The music and the air conditioner and my own golden voice had hidden the person's arrival. Resisting the burning in my leg, I rolled and came up with my .38.

But I stopped right there.

Rittle had an arm around Ada's chest; with his other hand he held something to her throat. Ada was pale as she struggled with her shock.

"Gun down," Rittle said in a voice from which the chumminess had run out like blood.

What he was pressing against her throat, I saw, was a knife, a dagger fashioned from milky green jade. The handle was carved in an intricate and ornate dragon. It was a beautiful and deadly piece of work. I lowered the gun.

"Easy," I said. "Let's talk about this."

He kicked the door closed, keeping the dagger where it was. He said: "This sucker slew enemies a thousand years ago, and it's just as sharp now as the day it was made."

Ada's eyes flicked across mine, then away. My blood was surging; it beat in my head, throbbed where the tendons in my knee were on fire. Sunlight coming through

231

the dusty jalousies hit the blade and bounced a smear of green reflection on the low ceiling.

"So that was the last piece of the collection," I said, to say it, to keep the moment from collapsing irrevocably on us all. "Khoy probably saved the dragon to sell separately. Which is why his prints were at Castle's. He'd gone there to pitch it. You went and got the other jade back, only Khoy never had sold the knife, and you wanted it. I see why. It's a piece of art."

"What tipped it?" Rittle demanded.

I saw an artery pulse in Ada's neck under the blade's edge. I swallowed. "Nothing big," I said. "I was pretty slow. When we found that newspaper in Khoy's apartment yesterday, you referred to Castle as 'the guy who died,' yet you showed up at his funeral, looking for Khoy. I saw your face in a photograph."

"Shit. I gave Castle's gorillas a trip to Boston to get them out of the way. The idea wasn't to kill him, just to get the stones. But he was there futzing around in his den, arrogant bastard, and suddenly it made sense. I'd already struck on a way to tie Khoy to everything. He did rip me off, the prick. Most people in those camps wait years for sponsors to cut the red tape to spring them. I worked it so he got cleared through ahead of others. He was gonna be my Stateside man. But he wrote and told me the stones never arrived, had a story about how they were seized by Thai customs. I didn't figure him for the rip-off till later, after he'd vanished—and after I knew he didn't get all his dough from you, darling." Rittle wrenched Ada's head and she gasped.

"Easy, man," I said. We all shifted position a little on the brown and gold tiles. My knee was blazing.

He was wound up, adrenaline-fueled. "I traced the others, figuring they could give me a line. But I didn't know if they knew about the jade or not, so why take risks? They even got their stories together, they could've put me in hurt. Tran was the last. It made sense Khoy would've been in touch with him. They were buddies."

"Did Bhuntan know?" Ada asked in a voice I almost did not hear. The knife was right there on her throat.

"Nah. And he wouldn't even confess he'd seen Khoy. But he had."

"You killed him," she rasped.

"Ada, don't," I said; I knew every word was costing her.

"You planted cocaine at his house!"

"Part of the setup. Like wearing the stocking when I went to your old lady's place," Rittle said to me. "I hung around town, biding my time, getting credible. Hell, I actually did some good in this city. Then I spotted Khoy at a Cambodian market. He saw me too and bolted. I tracked him to his rat hole on Broadway, but he was already smoke. I knew he wouldn't be around long. Ada's been impressed with you, Rasmussen. Hey, I never would've made that tinsel work."

I said, "The cop who questioned us last night told me no jade's been recovered. What'd you do, go back into the warehouse when I went to call them?"

"I got lucky. The stones were in one of the crates right by the dead chick. This beauty along with them," he said, tilting the dagger again, causing it to shine dully. "I stashed everything in the toolbox in my truck."

"You take the coke too?"

"I don't touch that shit. The jade is the point. I did my time, sticking my neck out in the war. I lost my marriage, my home. So I stayed over there afterwards."

"To help the needy," I said. "Good old Walt."

233

"I've got shrapnel in my back and shoulder. When do I get a reward for that?" He gave a tense smile and brandished the dagger. "I've got it now. You know what this stuff is worth? Time to make it all come up green, and I know how."

He reached over and flicked off the air conditioner, which died with a gurgle. "We'll go in your wheels, pal. You drive, Ada in the middle. Down the road there's a quarry. I'll take your gun now."

I envisioned one ending then. Someday long hence a curious scuba diver would find the antique Bobcat, a lace of rust in eighty feet of dark, still water, two skeletons inside, and the books would close on a mystery fifty years old, and by that time investigators and killer alike would long since have died and the Yunung-kash jade would have been bought and sold many times and still be as bright and shiny and priceless as it was right now. I shivered as though feeling the cold water already. I needed to invent a different ending.

I slid a painful half-step to the right. My knee was locking up, broken tendons curling back up inside like snipped cables. "Here it is," I said, pointing to the Masterpiece. "Take it."

Rittle didn't move. With the AC off, the coolness was evaporating. The sun blazed on the metal skin of the trailer and glinted on the edge of the dagger. We were all sweating.

"What've we got us?" he said. "A Texas-death standoff? You'll gun me all right, but Ada spurts her blood all over the floor and dies gagging." He forced her head back farther, exposing her throat. "Your move."

I edged another half-step to the right, trying not to wince. He turned, twisting Ada, keeping her between us.

It was chess with life-size pieces. My face was slick with sweat. "Haven't you figured out that I tipped the cops before I came here? Jeezum, Walt, you that dumb?"

He licked his lips and forced a smile, and I tried to decide which was real: the amiable, energetic little man? Or this perversity who had murdered seven people already? Would he let her live? "They're out there now," I said.

"Forget it. I saw you and the cops last night. Your fan club's small, Rasmussen." He angled the blade, and I saw a smear of blood on Ada's throat. Panic flickered in my mind.

"Put down the fucking gun!" he said.

I didn't want to; I was not where I wanted to be yet, but time was a string that had run out. Ada's life beat a membrane thickness from the green dragon. I bent to set the .38 on the parson's table, turning my shoulder to cut his view as I did. I gripped his tumbler, almost losing it as the wet glass squirmed in my sweaty fingers. But I had it. I swung my arm up in an arc, hurling tea, ice cubes, and then the glass, into his face.

Ada cried out once and tried to break away. Rittle recoiled, hanging on. As he brought the dagger up, I fired.

The round hit him high in the chest, the impact slamming him against the paneled wall, jolting the trailer, knocking his eyeglasses askew. The dagger clattered to the linoleum tiles. I did not fire again. He slid to the floor wearing a last look of enormous and useless surprise. Checkmate.

Ada reached for the dagger, then stopped and yanked back her hand. She gave a sob and threw herself into me, burrowing her face against my damp shirt to where my heart pounded. I set the .38 aside and held her for a long time.

34

⊘⊙⊘⊙⊘⊙⊘⊙⊘

THE SOIREE WAS SLATED for eight
P.M. at the International Institute. The doctor had gone
into my knee with an arthroscope. I was still limping, but
on the mend. Feeling spry I decided to walk from my office. As I cut across a big empty parking lot I saw three
kids shooting hoops at a rusty ring on a telephone pole.
The ball tipped off an outstretched hand and rolled my
way. I scooped it up, dribbled, and sank it from thirty feet
out. Bang. The kid who didn't faint grabbed the rebound
and flicked the ball back. I caught it.

"Man your size oughta be able to dunk it," the kid said,
a note of playground challenge in the way he did.

I said, "Catch me in the A.M. with coffee and a dough-
nut in my hand."

But, hell, I felt good. I put up the same shot, same crisp
roll off the fingertips, same clean arc. It missed by five feet.
The kid grinned and kept the ball this time.

I climbed through a neighborhood of swank apartment
buildings to High Street. Across town a train hooted happily. At the Father Norton Senior Center the old folks
were out front on the benches and in wheelchairs, doing
the last good thing left them: talking, enjoying it in a way
few people my side of decrepitude ever do. I waved. On

236

the street corner a pretty young Dominican woman, her features perked up with lipstick and rouge, waited for her swain, who arrived a moment later in a twenty-year-old convertible that gleamed like new, merengue pumping from its radio. In a doorway a middle-aged black man wearing a dated but well-brushed suit nodded at me and smiled. I had a sense, if not of true community, at least of people getting along on a Saturday night in summer.

The International Institute was alight and buzzing with guests. Francis X. was there in his TV suit and a tie like a striped kite, representing the department, glad-handing Southeast Asian community leaders, doing right by his family name as he carried on about how the Cambodians living in the city were a testament to the indomitability of the human spirit, not to mention how the LPD was there to guarantee protection for one and all. He watched me limp past without missing a beat.

I was able to look over the heads of most of the crowd. At the front of the hall, eight large-framed photographs were propped in a rainbow of chrysanthemums. One was of Bhuntan Tran and another was of Suoheang Khoy. Although there would be solemnity later, now there was a mood of festivity in the air. "Let be be finale of seem," Wallace Stevens had written. "The only emperor is the emperor of ice-cream." It seemed reasonable.

I spied Ada with an intense, good-looking man in a brown suit and tortoiseshell glasses. They were working the room slowly, talking here and there. She didn't see me, so I walked over and held up a wall. But every few seconds I filched a glance at Ada and felt myself grin like a madman on the inside.

We had had our conversation the afternoon following the events in Walter Rittle's trailer, after my knee surgery.

She finally told me the story of her brief marriage to Khoy. It had been part of her early attempt to save the world one leaky dike at a time. "It was also the last straw for my father," she said. "We'd been coming to that for a long time, I guess. The one lever he'd always had was the family money, which in truth neither my brother Chad nor I even cared about."

When I told her about having looked at her checkbook and bills that other morning, and about my conversation with Sydney Keyes at the antique gallery, Ada's expression darkened. "So you were suspicious of me."

What could I say?

"That must be a lousy way to be, Alex . . . to have become."

"Rotten, I admit it. But it wasn't all pink smoke. You omitted information in order to keep me hanging in there—you figured I'd drop the case otherwise."

She didn't deny it. But she also had never figured Khoy for being involved. The five thousand he supposedly had given to Tran actually came from Ada herself because, she said, she saw great promise in Tran. In wanting to see his name cleared after his death, she was protecting her investment. Of the man on the tape machine that other morning, she told me he was Trevor someone, a U.S. attorney she had met through refugee work and whom she had dated a few times when he got up to Boston on business. We had ended on an ambiguous note.

A registered check for the week's work plus a bonus had arrived two days ago, on Thursday. She had been out of town since, but I had known she would be here tonight.

"Bus don't stop here no more, mister."

I had no quip to top it. She was alone, finally. The white satin dress set off her hair and eyes, and I silently thanked old Charles Blaine Stewart for his taste in all things rare. She was to every other woman in the room what a diamond is to a crate of cubic zirconias. She held a white chrysanthemum in her hand. "How's your knee?"

"I'm walking. When did you get back?" I asked.

"This afternoon. It's been an intense week. How have you been?"

"Working."

"What a surprise." She laughed softly. She snapped most of the stem off the flower and arranged it in the buttonhole in my lapel. I felt fawned over.

"I got the check," I said, never at a loss for banter.

"You earned it. I've still got a few resources." She winked and took my hand and led me out to the portico in front of the building, away from the crowd. High overhead, cirrus clouds traced the last pinks of sunset.

"Walking, and working, and waiting too," I said, turning to her at the fence by the sidewalk. "I've missed you, lady. I'm glad you're back."

"That's what I wanted to talk to you about, Alex. You know I've been under it at work, starting to lose the old fire." She put a hand on the fence, instead of on me, which I took as not a good sign. "I got an offer this week. There's a staff opening on the Justice Department's committee on refugees."

"Washington?"

"Mostly, with some overseas travel."

"Well, it's a good opportunity, isn't it?"

She was watching me carefully. "I really would like to take it. I think I'm ready for change."

"Why not."

"There are private investigators in D.C. too, I hear tell."

"With all those honest politicians?"

Her smile had an unfamiliar strain. I lifted my shoulders and dropped them. "It's not an occupation that transfers easily," I said.

"What about one of the big law firms? They must use investigators. I've got some contacts. With some networking . . ." She saw my look and let the thought fade. "How about a security company?"

"Would I get to wear a patch on my sleeve?"

She dropped her eyes to her hand on the fence. Finally she looked up. "What would suit, Alex? Is there anything?"

I touched her shoulder and felt the tension there, alive and warm beneath my hand. If we could get away from here, right now, I thought. I glanced along the empty street for a cab.

"In my dictionary," I said, speaking carefully, "*network* is still a noun. To be halfway good at this job depends on knowing the streets, knowing which wheels can be greased, who can be leaned on. Knowing a cop or two doesn't hurt either. All that takes years if you're lucky."

"Like having friends?"

"That sometimes can be accomplished in a shorter time."

"I haven't noticed you've got many."

I met her eyes. "Two or three good ones are worth a cheering throng."

"You could have one very good friend in Washington," she said. She moved out from under my hand. "The real reason you wouldn't go is that file you showed me, isn't it?"

I felt the mood of expectancy caving in like sand being sucked away underfoot by a powerful wave that has crashed on shore and now has to return to where it came from. "There's a moon tonight," I said, pointing across rooftops to where it was rising fat and yellow.

"Sounds like an old love song," Ada said softly.

Silence hung for a moment, then she said, "Did you ever read *The Catcher in the Rye?*"

"That the one about the drunk ballplayer?"

"You accused me of having little Dutch kid disease, but you've got Caulfield Syndrome."

"Bad?"

"I saw you cover those photos of some nude young woman on your desk that first day."

"They could've been my private stash."

She shook her head. "I think about Holden trying to rub out the dirty words on the grammar school steps, wanting to keep the children safe, but realizing that if one were to spend a lifetime, he couldn't erase all the dirt in the world, all the hard truths."

"He's probably onto something there."

"So why do you try?"

"I might ask you the same. You went through a lot of trouble and risk to clear Bhuntan Tran."

"We're talking about you," Ada said. "Do you remember what happened to Holden?"

"Didn't end happily ever after, did he?"

"He cracked up."

"I'm not that complicated."

"That isn't the only fate that can befall you. There's frustration. Discouragement."

I'd taken a double major in them. "Yeah, well . . . "

"People can end up alone too," she said.

I let that one be, like a stone lying on the floor of my heart. Another stone must have stuck in my throat, because no words would come.

"I guess I knew what your reaction would be," Ada

went on quickly. "While I was in Washington I got another offer too."

"Two jobs?"

She shook her head. "Trevor."

"The voice on the phone."

"It happened kind of unexpectedly. He's getting a promotion. He'll be an advocate for people applying for citizenship, and we're both interested in that and he . . . he asked me to marry him."

"And you didn't say no?"

"He's looking for stability. I guess I am too. Funny, I've never really thought of myself that way, but I suppose I am. You can turn your back on your family, but in some part of you, you always know it's there. You get used to knowing that. I like the idea of Washington, but it's easy to get swamped in that town, especially alone. And I believe that together he and I can make a real difference."

"I thought we made a real difference here," I said. "Right here in this town."

"We did, and a lot of people are indebted to you, including me. Especially me."

"The hell with that," I said. "Tell the guy no. There're planes every day, and trains and cars. We could do this."

Ada swallowed. "Could we?"

Someone appeared at the doorway and said the program was starting. Ada took my arm in both her small hands and drew me farther away, along the brick wall toward the street. "If things had been different . . ." she said, "the timing, or . . ." She let it go and tried again. "The thing is, I don't meet many people like you, someone who's truly honest and responsible for himself, not needing a lot from others. Self-reliant."

"People have called it a failing."

"People who couldn't stand alone if their lives depended on it. I think Trevor is strong in his way, but he also needs me in a way I don't think you ever would."

"You don't know that."

We had stopped walking. Street lamps had come on, and when she turned to look at the door, I saw a wet gleam in her eyes. "No," she said, "I don't, and I guess I'll never find out. My loss." Her voice had thickened and she cleared her throat. "I don't imagine you want to meet him?"

"Guy in the brown suit?"

"Yes."

"I'll grant you that one."

"I've got to go, then. I'm supposed to make a little speech later."

"Another one?"

"Happier than this one, I hope," she said, and choked.

I didn't release her hand yet. "You're one of the honest ones too," I said. I kissed her forehead. "Remember to use first person plural in your home."

Her tears were rolling then, and she hooked them away with her thumb. "I won't forget you, Rasmussen."

"Who?"

She smiled brokenly, maybe gratefully, and hurried up the walk to the door. There was applause inside, which made it a good time to slip in, the way you do at church when you've come late. She was gone in an instant.

So I limped down High Street to East Merrimack and turned left. The moon turned too. Somewhere a train hooted, unhappy to be back in Lowell. In a laundromat a couple were folding a double bedsheet, which was a dance with steps all its own. I went past the repertory theater where Noël Coward's *Blithe Spirit* was running, and past the War Memorial Auditorium, and Chevy's Bel-Air Lounge. Inside Chevy's a mirrored globe was throwing splinters of color through the smoked windows. "I Only Have Eyes for You" was playing, the good old version by the Flamingoes, the voice of the lead singer floating languidly out onto the summer night. Boy, that brought me back to being a kid, which I definitely wasn't anymore. I felt ancient.

I walked across the Concord River flowing slick and black beneath my shoes, a few hundred yards away from losing itself forever in the bigger waters of the Merrimack. I took the chrysanthemum from my lapel, sniffed it, then dropped it and watched it slip under the bridge. I went past the federal building. Ahead, the sign atop the old *Sun* offices glowed high above the street. I could have got my car and gone back to the empty apartment, but I didn't want to just then. I wanted to stop by the office. Maybe there was a message on the tape, or someone in the waiting room who urgently needed my valuable services. A full moon did crazy things to people.

"Sha-bop sha-bop," I sang, for no good reason at all.